序 言

　　中級英語檢定考試中，有一項克漏字測驗，這項測驗考生最害怕，但卻是得分的關鍵。其實，只要練習，熟能生巧，克漏字測驗並沒有想像中困難。

　　克漏字測驗，不是考文法，就是考句意，原則上，四個選項完全不相同，就是考句意，要注意上下文意。若四個選項大致相同，只是詞類或是時態不相同，便是考文法。有時句意和文法同時考，其中的兩個選項是考句意，兩個選項是考文法。

　　「**中級英語克漏字測驗**」中的每一篇測驗，均附有翻譯及註釋，對錯答案都有明確的交待，讀者可以快速地閱讀，節省查字典的時間。學習出版公司編書的一貫原則，就是確確實實，絕不避重就輕，像這本書，編寫起來很花功夫，有時為了一條題目的對錯答案，經由好幾位中外老師討論後，才能決定，**務必使書中每個答案絕對正確**。

　　本書編輯校對嚴謹，但恐仍有些微疏漏，祈盼各界先進不吝指正。

劉　毅

本書製作過程

　　本書 Test 2、4、6、8、10、13、16、17、26、41、42、43、49、50 由廖曄嵐老師命題，Test 12 及 Test 15 由李建琴老師命題，Test 19 及 Test 44～48 由唐慧莊老師命題，Test 1、3、5、7、9、11、14、15、18、20～25、27～40 由謝靜芳老師負責。命題後，詳解由謝靜芳老師執筆。全書完成後，先由命題老師校對完，又請 Andy Swarzman、Ted Pigott、Bill Allen 三位外籍老師詳細校對。全部測驗題均經過劉毅英文家教班三千多位同學實際測驗過，同學的克漏字解題能力有顯著的提升。

本書另附有學生用書，售價 100 元。

TEST 1

Read the following passage, and choose the best answer for each blank.

There was a serious accident in the chemistry lab last week. A confused student accidentally poured a wrong mixture of ___1___ in a test tube. There was a strong explosion. ___2___ pieces of glass from the test tube flew in all directions. A piece of flying glass found ___3___ mark in John Chen's right arm. The lab instructor saw blood ___4___ from John's arm. He immediately ___5___ the university's infirmary about the accident.

1. A. chemicals
   B. chemistry
   C. chemists
   D. chemism

2. A. Breaking
   B. Break
   C. Broke
   D. Broken

3. A. its
   B. it's
   C. their
   D. his

4. A. trickling
   B. trickled
   C. bled
   D. bleeds

5. A. cancelled
   B. talked
   C. notified
   D. recalled

TEST 1 詳解

There was a serious accident *in the chemistry lab* *last week*. A
confused student *accidentally* poured a wrong mixture *of chemicals*
$\overline{}$
                                                                    1
in a test tube. There was a strong explosion. <u>Broken</u> pieces *of glass*
                                                        2
from the test tube flew *in all directions*.

上星期，化學實驗室發生了嚴重的意外事件。有個迷糊的學生，誤將一些
混錯的化學藥品倒入試管中，造成了劇烈的爆炸。試管的玻璃碎片四處飛散。

> chemistry〔'kɛmɪstrɪ〕*n.* 化學　　lab〔læb〕*n.* 實驗室（= *laboratory*）
> confused〔kən'fjuzd〕*adj.* 困惑的
> accidentally〔͵æksə'dɛntḷɪ〕*adv.* 意外地　　pour〔por〕*v.* 傾倒
> mixture〔'mɪkstʃɚ〕*n.* 混合　　*test tube* 試管

1. (**A**) (A) ***chemical***〔'kɛmɪkḷ〕*n.* 化學藥品
　　　　　(B) chemistry〔'kɛmɪstrɪ〕*n.* 化學
　　　　　(C) chemist〔'kɛmɪst〕*n.* 化學家
　　　　　(D) chemism〔'kɛmɪzəm〕*n.* 化學作用

2. (**D**) 依句意，選 (D) ***broken***〔'brokən〕*adj.* 破碎的。過去分詞表「被動、
　　　　　完成」。而 (A) breaking 爲現在分詞，表「主動、進行」，作「正在破
　　　　　裂的」解，不合乎句意。

A piece *of flying glass* found <u>its</u> mark *in John Chen's right arm*.
                                       3
The lab instructor saw blood *trickling from John's arm*. He *imme-*
                                    4
diately <u>notified</u> the university's infirmary about the accident.
         5

有一片飛舞的碎片，刺到陳約翰的右手臂。實驗室的講師看到血從約翰的手臂上流出來。他立刻通知學校的保健室。

> find〔faɪnd〕*v.* 自然成為　　mark〔mɑrk〕*n.* 疤痕
> instructor〔ɪn'strʌktɚ〕*n.* 講師
> infirmary〔ɪn'fɜmərɪ〕*n.* 保健室

3. (**A**) it 代替不可數名詞 glass，its「它的」為其所有格。

4. (**A**) 感官動詞 see 接受詞之後，接現在分詞表動作正在進行，故選 (A) ***trickling***。

　　trickle〔'trɪk!〕*v.* 滴下；細細地流
　　bleed〔blid〕*v.* 流血（三態變化：bleed – bled – bled）

5. (**C**) (A) cancel〔'kæns!〕*v.* 取消
　　　　(B) talk〔tɔk〕*v.* 談話
　　　　(C) ***notify***〔'notə,faɪ〕*v.* 通知
　　　　(D) recall〔rɪ'kɔl〕*v.* 記起
　　　根據句意，選 (C)。

TEST 2

Read the following passage, and choose the best answer for each blank.

Happiness is a shy ___1___. If you hunt it, it will fly away. It is better to set a trap for it and look ___2___ way. Pleasure-seekers miss it. They are restless, discontented people, who, ___3___ no inward happiness, seek it in outward things, ___4___ they do not often find it. It is a common mistake ___5___ that money brings happiness. "If only I ___6___ rich!" we sigh. Money is not to be despised, and it can do much to ___7___ life pleasant. Yet ___8___ are sometimes unhappy, and some poor men sing. So the ___9___ of happiness cannot be simply in wealth, and ___10___ those who will never be rich can still be happy.

1. A. dog
   B. cat
   C. bird
   D. pig

2. A. other
   B. the other
   C. another
   D. others

3. A. have
   B. has
   C. having
   D. had

4. A. which
   B. that
   C. what
   D. where

5. A. to think
   B. think
   C. thought
   D. thinks

6. A. am
   B. is
   C. were
   D. was

7. A. let
   B. make
   C. have
   D. cause

8. A. rich
   B. riches
   C. the rich
   D. the riches

9. A. source
   B. resource
   C. course
   D. reason

10. A. almost
    B. even
    C. nearly
    D. only

TEST 2 詳解

Happiness is a shy <u>bird</u>. *If you hunt it*, it will fly *away*.
　　　　　　　　　1

It is better to set a trap *for it* **and** look <u>the other</u> way.
　　　　　　　　　　　　　　　　　　　　　　2

　　快樂是隻害羞的小鳥。如果你獵捕牠，牠會飛走。最好給牠設個圈套，而眼觀他方。

> shy〔ʃaɪ〕*adj.* 害羞的　　hunt〔hʌnt〕*v.* 狩獵；追逐
> set〔sɛt〕*v.* 設置　　trap〔træp〕*n.* 陷阱
> ***set a trap for*** 設陷阱捕捉~

1. (**C**) 由句意可知，只有「鳥」會飛走，故選 (C) ***bird*** 。

2. (**B**) 依句意，選 (B) ***look the other way*** 「看另一邊」。the other 指「兩者中的另一個」。而 (A) other 「其他的」後接複數名詞，(C) another 「(三者以上的)另一個」，(D) others 是代名詞，表「其他的人；其他的東西」，用法與句意均不合。

Pleasure-seekers miss it. They are restless, discontented people,

who, *having no inward happiness*, seek it *in outward things*, *where*
　　　3　　　　　　　　　　　　　　　　　　　　　　　　　　　　4

they do not often find it.

　　尋歡作樂的人抓不到牠。他們是坐立不安，感到不滿的人，因為他們沒有內在的快樂，而想在外在的事物中尋找快樂，卻常找不到。

> pleasure-seeker〔'plɛʒɚ,sikɚ〕*n.* 尋歡作樂的人　　miss〔mɪs〕*v.* 沒有抓住
> restless〔'rɛstlɪs〕*adj.* 坐立不安的
> discontented〔,dɪskən'tɛntɪd〕*adj.* 不滿的
> inward〔'ɪnwəd〕*adj.* 內在的；精神的
> outward〔'aʊtwəd〕*adj.* 外在的；物質的

3. (**C**) who seek it in outward things 為形容詞子句，修飾其先行詞 people。而 ***having*** no inward happiness 則是由副詞子句 because they have no inward happiness 簡化而來的分詞片語。

4. (**D**) 空格應填一表地點的關係副詞，故選 (D) ***where*** (= *in which*)。 原句為：…they do not often find it in outward things.
　　　　　　　　　　　　　　　　　　　　　 ‖
　　　　　　　　　　　　　　　　　　　　　 which

It is a common mistake <u>to think</u> ***that*** money brings happiness.
　　　　　　　　　　　　 5

"***If only*** I <u>were</u> rich!" we sigh. Money is not to be despised, ***and***
　　　　　　　　　 6

it can do much to <u>make</u> life pleasant. ***Yet*** <u>the rich</u> are *sometimes*
　　　　　　　　　 7　　　　　　　　　　　　 8

unhappy, ***and*** some poor men sing.

認為金錢會帶來快樂，這是常見的錯誤。我們嘆息著說：「但願我有錢！」金錢 是不該被瞧不起，而且在使生活舒適這一方面，非常有用。然而有錢人有時也 會不快樂，而有些窮人卻很快樂。

　　common〔'kɑmən〕*adj.* 普通的；常見的　　despise〔dɪ'spaɪz〕*v.* 瞧不起
　　pleasant〔'plɛznt〕*adj.* 快樂的　　sing〔sɪŋ〕*v.* 感到歡樂

5. (**A**) it 置於句首做虛主詞，以代替後面的真主詞，如不定詞、動名詞片 語，或 that 子句，故選 (A) ***to think***。

6. (**C**) If only ~ = I wish ~ 表「但願…」，為假設語氣，依句意為與現 在事實相反的假設，故動詞須用過去式，be 動詞則一律用 ***were***。

7. (**B**) 「make + 受詞 + 受詞補語 (形容詞、過去分詞或名詞)」，表「使~…」， 故選 (B)。而 (A) let，(C) have 均為使役動詞，其用法為：「let / have + 受詞 + 原形 V.」；而 (D) cause「使~」為一般動詞，其用法為： 「cause + 受詞 + to V.」，用法均不合。

8. (**C**)「the + 形容詞」= 複數名詞 *the rich* 有錢人（= *the rich people*）

So the source *of happiness* cannot be *simply* in wealth, *and*
9

even those *who will never be rich* can *still* be happy.
10

所以快樂的來源不是只來自於財富，而甚至那些永遠都不會有錢的人，仍舊能感受快樂。

wealth〔wɛlθ〕*n.* 財富

9. (**A**) 依句意，選 (A) *source*〔sors〕*n.* 來源。而 (B) resource〔rɪˋsors〕*n.* 資源，(C) course〔kors〕*n.* 課程，(D) reason〔ˋrizn〕*n.* 理由，均不合句意。

10. (**B**) 依句意，選 (B) *even*「甚至」。而 (A) almost = (C) nearly「幾乎」，(D) 只有，則不合句意。

TEST 3

Read the following passage, and choose the best answer for each blank.

Fishing in America is really __1__ most of the time.
During weekends most of the fishing fanatics are in pursuit
of this __2__. But according to the rule of the American
government, those who fish are required to have fishing
__3__. However, in fact, almost __4__ of them do not
have one. If these people cannot show the permit, when
asked, they will be given __5__.

1. A. empty
   B. enjoyable
   C. interested
   D. bored

2. A. player
   B. distance
   C. hunting
   D. outdoor fun

3. A. ambition
   B. books
   C. licenses
   D. approve

4. A. one third
   B. one thirds
   C. one three
   D. two third

5. A. a praise
   B. a fine
   C. an award
   D. a reward

TEST 3 詳解

Fishing *in America* is *really* enjoyable *most of the time.*
1

During weekends most *of the fishing fanatics* are in pursuit of this

outdoor fun. ***But*** *according to the rule of the American government,*
2

those ***who fish*** are required to have fishing licenses. *However, in*
3

fact, almost one third of them do not have one. *If these people*
4

cannot show the permit, ***when*** *asked,* they will be given a fine.
5

通常在美國釣魚眞是一件很愉快的事。週末時,大部分釣魚迷都在從事這種戶外的娛樂。但根據美國政府的規定,釣客必須要有釣魚執照。然而,事實上,幾乎三分之一的釣客都沒有許可證。如果這些人被查問時,拿不出許可證的話,就會被罰款。

fanatic〔fə'nætɪk〕*n.* 狂熱者   pursuit〔pə'sut〕*n.* 追求;從事
require〔rɪ'kwaɪr〕*v.* 需要   ***be required to*** 必須~
permit〔'pɝmɪt〕*n.* 許可證

1. (**B**) (A) 空的   (B) ***enjoyable***〔ɪn'dʒɔɪəbl̩〕*adj.* 愉快的
      (C) 感興趣的   (D) 無聊的

2. (**D**) (A) 選手   (B) distance〔'dɪstəns〕*n.* 距離
      (C) 打獵   (D) ***outdoor fun*** 戶外娛樂

3. (**C**)　(A) ambition〔æm'bɪʃən〕*n.* 野心；抱負
　　　　　(C) ***license***〔'laɪsṇs〕*n.* 執照
　　　　　(D) approve〔ə'pruv〕*v.* 贊成

4. (**A**)　分數的表達法：分子用基數（即 one, two, three, …），分母用序數（即 first, second, third, …）。當分子大於 2 時，分母須加 s，故「三分之一」應寫成 ***one third***，選 (A)。

5. (**B**)　(A) praise〔prez〕*n.* 稱讚
　　　　　(B) ***fine***〔faɪn〕*n.* 罰款
　　　　　(C) award〔ə'wɔrd〕*n.* 獎；獎品
　　　　　(D) reward〔rɪ'wɔrd〕*n.* 報酬；獎賞

TEST 4

Read the following passage, and choose the best answer for each blank.

Many countries of the world celebrate Mother's Day at different times and __1__ different ways. In the West, the earliest __2__ Mother's Day celebrations were held in ancient Greece __3__ Rhea, the Mother of the Gods.

England in the 1600s celebrated a day __4__ Mothering Sunday. At that time, many of England's poor __5__ servants for the wealthy, and most servants had the day __6__ to travel, often long distances, to be with their mothers.

In the United States, Mother's Day was first suggested in 1872 as a day __7__ to peace. In 1907, Ann Jarvis of Philadelphia began a __8__ to establish a national Mother's Day. She was finally __9__ in 1914, when President Woodrow Wilson __10__ Mother's Day a national holiday to be held on the second Sunday of May every year.

1. A. by
   B. in
   C. with
   D. to

2. A. know
   B. knew
   C. known
   D. knowing

3. A. in honor of
   B. in the light of
   C. in terms of
   D. in return for

4. A. which calls
   B. that is called
   C. called
   D. calling

5. A. work with
   B. worked as
   C. working for
   D. to work

6. A. off
   B. up
   C. down
   D. by

7. A. dedicate
   B. dedication
   C. dedicated
   D. dedicating

8. A. champagne
   B. campaign
   C. congratulation
   D. career

9. A. succeed
   B. succeeded
   C. successful
   D. success

10. A. proclaimed
    B. claimed
    C. exclaimed
    D. explained

TEST 4 詳解

Many countries *of the world* celebrate Mother's Day *at*

different times **and** *in different ways.* *In the West*, the earliest
___
1

known Mother's Day celebrations were held *in ancient Greece*
___
2

in honor of Rhea, the Mother of the Gods.
___
3

世界上有許多國家，在不同的時間，以不同的方式慶祝母親節。就我們所知，西方最早的母親節慶祝活動，是在古希臘舉行，當初是爲了要紀念衆神之母麗亞。

hold〔hold〕*v.* 舉行　　ancient〔'enʃənt〕*adj.* 古代的
celebration〔,sɛlə'breʃən〕*n.* 慶祝活動　　Greece〔gris〕*n.* 希臘

1. (**B**) *in ~ way* 以～方式

2. (**C**) 以句意，「爲大家所熟知的」母親節慶祝活動，故選 (C) *known*
〔non〕*adj.* 衆所周知的。而 (D) knowing〔'noɪŋ〕*adj.* 聰明的，則不合句意。

3. (**A**) (A) *in honor of ~* 爲了紀念～
(B) in the light of ~ 從～觀點來看
(C) in terms of ~ 從～觀點來看
(D) in return for ~ 爲了回報～

England *in the 1600s* celebrated a day *called Mothering*
　　　　　　　　　　　　　　　　　　　　　　4

Sunday. *At that time,* many *of England's poor* worked as servants
　　　　　　　　　　　　　　　　　　　　　　　5

for the wealthy, **and** most servants had the day off to travel,
　　　　　　　　　　　　　　　　　　　　　　　　6

often long distances, *to be with their mothers.*

十七世紀時，英國有個節日叫「拜望雙親日」。那時英國有很多窮人在有錢人家幫傭，在「拜望雙親日」那天，他們會放假一天，常常是經過長途跋涉之後，才回到家跟母親團聚。

Mothering Sunday 拜望雙親日（按照英國農俗指四旬齋第四個星期日）
poor〔pur〕*n.* 窮人　　servant〔'sɜvənt〕*n.* 傭人
the wealthy 有錢人　distance〔'dɪstəns〕*n.* 距離；路程

4. (**C**) 原句是由 ⋯ a day which was called Mothering Sunday. 省略 which was 簡化而來。

5. (**B**) **work as** a servant 擔任傭人的工作

6. (**A**) have a day **off** 休假一天

In the United States, Mother's Day was *first* suggested *in*
1872 as a day *dedicated to peace.* *In 1907,* Ann Jarvis of
　　　　　　　　　　　　7

Philadelphia began a campaign to establish a national Mother's
　　　　　　　　　　　8

Day. She was *finally* successful *in 1914,* **when** President Woodrow
　　　　　　　　　　　　9

Wilson proclaimed Mother's Day a national holiday to be held on
　　　　　10

the second Sunday of May every year.

美國在一八七二年時，有人建議以紀念和平之名，創立母親節。一九○七年，來自費城的安・賈維斯，開始提倡將母親節訂為國定紀念日。一九一四年，她的努力終於獲得成功，由當時的威爾遜總統宣佈，每年五月的第二個星期天為國定假日母親節。

Philadelphia〔ˌfɪləˈdɛlfɪə〕*n.* 費城

7. (**C**) *be dedicated to ~* 獻給~；為紀念~
原句是由… as a day which was dedicated to peace. 簡化而來。

8. (**B**) 依句意，選 (B) *campaign*〔kæmˈpen〕*n.* 活動；運動。
而 (A) champagne〔ʃæmˈpen〕*n.* 香檳酒，(C) congratulation〔kənˌgrætʃəˈleʃən〕*n.* 祝賀，(D) career〔kəˈrɪr〕*n.* 職業；生涯，均不合句意。

9. (**C**) 因前有 be 動詞，故空格應填形容詞，故選 (C) *successful*「成功的」。
而 (A) succeed〔səkˈsid〕*v.* 成功；繼承，(D) success〔səkˈsɛs〕*n.* 成功，用法均不合。

10. (**A**) (A) *proclaim*〔proˈklem〕*v.* 宣佈
(B) claim〔klem〕*v.* 要求
(C) exclaim〔ɪkˈsklem〕*v.* 呼喊
(D) explain〔ɪkˈsplen〕*v.* 解釋

TEST 5

Read the following passage, and choose the best answer for each blank.

Although the credit card system makes ___1___ easier shopping and managing of money, there is an important feature which is often ___2___ by unwise credit card users. With a credit card you have to handle your expenses far more carefully ___3___ you only used cash. In order not to get into debt over your head, you must ___4___ an account of what you will have to pay. Unfortunately, many credit card users fall into the trap of "spending now and worrying about it ___5___."

1. A. up
   B. at
   C. out
   D. for

2. A. ignored
   B. inspected
   C. heeded
   D. appreciated

3. A. than
   B. than if
   C. as if
   D. if

4. A. take
   B. make
   C. keep
   D. do

5. A. late
   B. later
   C. latter
   D. lately

TEST 5 詳解

Although the credit card system makes *for* easier shopping
                                         1
and managing *of money,* there is an important feature *which is*

often *ignored* by unwise credit card users. *With a credit card* you
        2
have to handle your expenses *far more carefully* *than if* you only
                                                      3
used cash.

雖然信用卡制度，使購物和管理金錢更為容易，但是有一項重要的特點，
卻常常被不明智的持卡人所忽略。和只使用現金比起來，有了信用卡，你就必
須更加小心處理你的開銷。

> *credit card* 信用卡　　manage〔'mænɪdʒ〕*v.* 管理
> feature〔'fitʃɚ〕*n.* 特點　　handle〔'hændl̩〕*v.* 處理
> expense〔ɪk'spɛns〕*n.* 花費　　cash〔kæʃ〕*n.* 現金

1. (**D**) (A) make up 編造；組成　　(B) make at 攻擊
   (C) make out 理解　　(D) *make for* 有助於

2. (**A**) (A) *ignore*〔ɪg'nor〕*v.* 忽略　　(B) inspect〔ɪn'spɛkt〕*v.* 檢查
   (C) heed〔hid〕*v.* 注意
   (D) appreciate〔ə'priʃɪ‚et〕*v.* 欣賞；感激

3. (**B**) 由句中 more 可知，應選含有比較級的連接詞，且依句意，選 (B) *than*
   if。原句為… *than* (you handle your expenses) *if* you only
   used cash. 而 (C) as if「就好像」，(D) 如果，文法與句意均不合。

In order not to get into debt over your head, you must keep an

₄

account *of what you will have to pay. Unfortunately*, many credit

card users fall into the trap *of "spending now and worrying about*

it later."

₅

為了避免負債過頭了，你必須把應付的款項記錄下來。不幸的是，許多持卡人都掉進了「先花費、後擔心」的陷阱中。

> **get into debt** 負債　　**over one's head** 超過某人的能力；過頭
> trap〔træp〕*n.* 陷阱

4. (**C**) **keep an account of** 記錄

5. (**B**) 依句意，應選與 now 相對應的 (B) **later**〔'letɚ〕*adv.* 以後。
　　而 (A) late〔let〕*adj.* 遲的；晚的，(C) latter〔'lætɚ〕*adj.* 後者的，
　　(D) lately〔'letlɪ〕*adv.* 最近，均不合句意。

TEST 6

Read the following passage, and choose the best answer for each blank.

So many people ___1___ up, rush to get ready, grab a cup of coffee, and charge out the door to work. After ___2___ all day, they return home, ___3___. The same is usually true for men and women who stay home with their children: They get up just ___4___ time to start doing things for the kids. There is virtually no time for anything else. Whether you work, raise a family, or both, ___5___ the most part you are too tired to enjoy any time ___6___ for you. As a solution ___7___ the tiredness, the assumption is often ___8___, "I'd better get as much sleep as I can." So your free time is spent ___9___. For many people this creates a deep longing in the heart. Surely there must be more to life ___10___ work, children, and sleep!

1. A. awake
   B. awaken
   C. wake
   D. woke

2. A. work
   B. works
   C. working
   D. worked

3. A. tire
   B. tired
   C. tiring
   D. tiredness

4. A. in
   B. for
   C. by
   D. at

5. A. for
   B. in
   C. to
   D. on

6. A. leave
   B. leaving
   C. left
   D. leaves

7. A. for
   B. to
   C. with
   D. in

8. A. done
   B. made
   C. played
   D. talked

9. A. sleep
   B. sleeping
   C. slept
   D. asleep

10. A. as
    B. than
    C. then
    D. like

TEST 6 詳解

So many people <u>wake</u> up, rush to get ready, grab a cup of
1

coffee, ***and*** charge out the door *to work*. *After working all day*,
2

they return home, <u>tired</u>.
3

有很多人一起床就匆忙梳洗，匆忙喝杯咖啡，就衝出門去上班。工作一整
天後，再拖著疲憊的身體回家。

rush ﹝ rʌʃ ﹞ v. 匆忙　　grab ﹝ græb ﹞ v. 急抓；匆忙地做
charge ﹝ tʃɑrdʒ ﹞ v. 向前衝

1. (**C**) 依句意，為現在簡單式，故選 (C)。　　***wake up*** 醒來
(D) woke 為 wake 的過去式，故不合。而 (A) awake ﹝ ə'wek ﹞ vi. 醒
來 (= *wake up*)　vt. 喚醒 (睡著的人)，(B) awaken ﹝ ə'wekən ﹞ vt.
喚醒；使覺悟；使察覺到，用法與句意均不合。

2. (**C**) after 為介系詞，其後須接名詞或動名詞，依句意，選 (C) ***working*** 。
而 (A) after work「下班後」，為一副詞片語，表時間，其後不可
接 all day，故不合。

3. (**B**) 空格應填一補語，補充說明主詞 they 的狀態，依句意，「覺得疲倦
的」，選 (B) ***tired*** 。而 (A) tire ﹝ taɪr ﹞ v. 使疲倦，(C) tiring ﹝'taɪrɪŋ ﹞
adj. 令人疲倦的，(D) tiredness ﹝'taɪrdnɪs ﹞ n. 疲倦，均不合句意。

The same is *usually* true for men and women ***who*** *stay home with*

their children: They get up *just in time to start doing things for*
4

the kids. There is *virtually* no time for anything else. ***Whether***

you work, raise a family, or both, for the most part you are too
　　　　　　　　　　　　　　　　　　5

tired to enjoy any time *left for you.*
　　　　　　　　　　　6

留在家裏照顧小孩的人也一樣：一起床就開始張羅小孩的事，幾乎沒有時間做別的。不論是上班族，還是負責養育子女的人，或者兩者都是，可能大多累得無法享受任何剩餘的時間了。

　　　virtually〔'vɝtʃʊəlɪ〕 *adv.* 幾乎　　　raise〔rez〕 *v.* 養育

4. (**A**) *in time* 及時；剛好來得及

5. (**A**) *for the most part* 大部分；大多（ = *mostly* ）

6. (**C**) 原句是由… any time *that is left* for you 省略關代 that 與 be
動詞 is 簡化而來。

As a solution to the tiredness, the assumption is *often* made, "I'd
　　　　　　　7　　　　　　　　　　　　　　　　　　8

better get *as* much sleep *as I can." So* your free time is spent

sleeping. *For many people* this creates a deep longing *in the*
　9

heart. *Surely* there must be more to life *than* work, *children,*
　　　　　　　　　　　　　　　　　　　10

and sleep!

疲倦時，一般認爲解決辦法通常是：「我最好多睡一點。」所以，你的空閒時間都花在睡眠上。對許多人來說，這使他們的內心產生了一種強烈的渴望。人生當然應該不只是工作、孩子和睡眠吧！

　　　assumption〔ə'sʌmpʃən〕 *n.* 假定　　　*free time* 空閒時間
　　　deep〔dip〕 *adj.* 極度的；強烈的　　　longing〔'lɔŋɪŋ〕 *n.* 渴望

7. (**B**) *a solution to* ～ ～的解決之道

8. (**B**) *make an assumption* 作個假定

9. (**B**) spend + 時間 + (in) + V-ing 「花時間～」　本句為被動語態，用
法為「時間 + be spent + (in) + V-ing」，故選 (B) *sleeping*。

10. (**B**) *more than* 不只是

TEST 7

Read the following passage, and choose the best answer for each blank.

When I was employed by a private corporation and assigned to the space-shuttle program, ___1___ ordering supplies. One of the engineers asked me to get a new dictionary for him. The request form said, "State reason this item is needed," so I asked him ___2___ he wanted one.

I expected his answer would be "My old ___3___ is lost." or "The cover is falling off." ___4___, he replied, "My edition ___5___ 'spaceship' as 'an imaginary aircraft.'" He got his new dictionary.

1. A. my job was included in
   B. my job included
   C. and my job was including
   D. my job including

2. A. when
   B. whether
   C. why
   D. where

3. A. copy
   B. order
   C. job
   D. assignment

4. A. Instead
   B. Therefore
   C. Moreover
   D. In addition

5. A. explains
   B. refines
   C. believes
   D. defines

TEST 7 詳解

When I was employed by a private corporation *and* assigned

to the space-shuttle program, my job included ordering supplies.
                                    —————————————
                                          1

One *of the engineers* asked me to get a new dictionary *for him.*

The request form said, "State reason *this item is needed,*" *so* I

asked him *why* he wanted one.
           ———
            2

　　我受雇於一家私人公司時，被指派到太空梭計劃部門，我的工作包括訂購
補給品。有位工程師要我替他買一本新的字典。由於申購單上面寫著：「請敘
述該物品需要的理由。」所以我就問他爲什麼需要新的字典。

employ〔ɪm'plɔɪ〕*v.* 雇用　　corporation〔͵kɔrpə'reʃən〕*n.* 公司
assign〔ə'saɪn〕*v.* 指派　*space shuttle* 太空梭
order〔'ɔrdɚ〕*v.* 訂購　　supplies〔sə'plaɪz〕*n. pl.* 補給品
request form 申購單　　state〔stet〕*v.* 敘述
item〔'aɪtəm〕*n.* 項目；物品

1.(**B**)　空格前是一個由 when 所引導的副詞子句，其後應接主要子句，故選
　　　　(B) *my job included* 。而 (A) 爲被動語態，不合句意；(C) 中出現連
　　　　接詞 and，應去掉；(D) 用分詞構句，造成本句缺乏主要子句，故不合。

2.(**C**)　由於申購單上已標明要敘述申購的理由，所以作者會問工程師「爲何」
　　　　需要字典，選 (C) *why* 。

I expected his answer would be "My old <u>copy</u> is lost." ***or***
　　　　　　　　　　　　　　　　　　　　　　3

"The cover is falling off." <u>*Instead*</u>, he replied, "My edition <u>defines</u>
　　　　　　　　　　　　　　　　4　　　　　　　　　　　　　　　　5

'spaceship' as "an imaginary aircraft." He got his new dictionary.

　　我以為他的回答會是：「我舊的那本遺失了。」或「它的封面脫落了。」
相反地，他卻回答：「我的那本把『太空船』定義為一種想像的飛行器。」於
是他就得到了一本新字典。

> ***fall off*** 脫落　　edition〔ɪˈdɪʃən〕*n.* 版本
> spaceship〔ˈspesˌʃɪp〕*n.* 太空船
> imaginary〔ɪˈmædʒəˌnɛrɪ〕*adj.* 想像的
> aircraft〔ˈɛrˌkræft〕*n.* 飛行器；飛機

3. (**A**) 任何印刷品或書籍的「一本」，都可以用 copy 來表示。
　　　　而 (B) 訂購，(C) 工作，(D) 作業，均不合句意。

4. (**A**) 空格前後有表示相反的情形，中間需一轉承語，表「相反地；取而代
　　　　之」，故選 (A) ***Instead*** 。
　　　　而 (B) 因此，(C) 而且，(D) 此外，均不合句意。

5. (**D**) ***define*** A ***as*** B 把 A 定義為 B
　　　　而 (A) 解釋，(B) refine〔rɪˈfaɪn〕*v.* 精煉，(C) 相信，均不合句意。

TEST 8

Read the following passage, and choose the best answer for each blank.

You've been to Yangmingshan and seen the cherry blossoms there, __1__ you? Well, back in 1885, Eliza Scidmore, an American writer and photographer, __2__ to Japan. She saw the cherry blossoms in Tokyo and admired them very much.

At that time, Washington, D.C. was a __3__ city and new land __4__ reclaimed from the Potomac River. This area was ugly and Scidmore thought that cherry trees would __5__ it up.

For twenty-five years the city __6__ her idea. They said people would climb the trees and break them. Finally, in 1912 the city of Tokyo __7__ 3,000 trees to Washington. Eliza was __8__. Now the cherry blossoms are one of Washington's most famous __9__ — just like they __10__ on Yangmingshan.

1. A. aren't
   B. don't
   C. didn't
   D. haven't

2. A. have been
   B. has gone
   C. went
   D. had been

3. A. rapid-growing
   B. rapidly-grown
   C. rapidly-growing
   D. rapid-grown

4. A. had been
   B. has been
   C. will be
   D. would be

5. A. show
   B. turn
   C. brighten
   D. wake

6. A. refused
   B. has refused
   C. was refusing
   D. would refuse

7. A. devoted
   B. donated
   C. owed
   D. dedicated

8. A. delighted
   B. delightful
   C. pleasing
   D. pleasant

9. A. health resorts
   B. historic sites
   C. amusement parks
   D. tourist attractions

10. A. were
    B. are
    C. did
    D. do

TEST 8 詳解

You've been to Yangmingshan **and** seen the cherry blossoms there, haven't you? Well, *back in 1885*, Eliza Scidmore, *an*
$\underset{1}{\underline{\text{haven't}}}$

American writer and photographer, $\underset{2}{\underline{\text{went}}}$ to Japan. She saw the

cherry blossoms *in Tokyo* **and** admired them *very much*.

你去過陽明山，也在那裏看過櫻花，不是嗎？嗯，在一八八五年的時候，有位美國作家兼攝影師伊麗莎·西得摩，前往日本。她在東京看見了櫻花，並對櫻花大為讚賞。

cherry (ˈtʃɛrɪ) *n.* 櫻桃；櫻桃樹　　blossom (ˈblɑsəm) *n.* 花
cherry blossoms 櫻花　　photographer (fəˈtɑgrəfə) *n.* 攝影師
admire (ədˈmaɪr) *v.* 讚賞

1. (**D**) 由於前面的助動詞是 have，且為肯定句，故附加問句用 "***haven't*** you?"，選 (D)。

2. (**C**) 依句意為過去式，選 (C) ***went***。

At that time, Washington, D.C. was a $\underset{3}{\underline{\text{rapidly-growing}}}$ city

and new land $\underset{4}{\underline{\text{had been}}}$ reclaimed *from the Potomac River*. This

area was ugly **and** Scidmore thought **that** *cherry trees would*

$\underset{5}{\underline{\text{brighten}}}$ *it up*.

當時華盛頓特區是個成長十分快速的都市，在波多馬克河塡土後，獲得了新的土地。這個地區十分醜陋，而西得摩認爲櫻桃樹會使它鮮亮生色。

reclaim〔rɪ'klem〕v. 開墾；塡土　　ugly〔'ʌglɪ〕adj. 醜的

3. (**C**) 依句意，選 (C) *rapidly-growing* 「快速成長的」。

4. (**A**) 依句意爲過去式，而且塡土的動作也已完成，故選 (A) *had been*。

5. (**C**) (A) show up 出現
　　　　　(B) turn up 開大聲
　　　　　(C) *brighten up* 使鮮亮生色
　　　　　(D) wake up 叫醒

For twenty-five years the city refused her idea. They said
　　　　　　　　　　　　　　　　6
people would climb the trees **and** *break them.* Finally, *in 1912*

the city of Tokyo donated 3,000 trees to Washington. Eliza
　　　　　　　　　7
was delighted. *Now* the cherry blossoms are one *of Washington's*
　　　8
most famous tourist attractions—*just like they are on Yangmingshan.*
　　　　　　　　　　　9　　　　　　　　　　10

　二十五年來，華盛頓特區一直不肯採納她的意見。他們認爲人們會爬上櫻桃樹，並加以破壞。最後在一九一二年，東京捐了三千棵櫻桃樹給華盛頓特區。伊麗莎非常高興。現在櫻花是華盛頓最著名的觀光名勝之一——就像陽明山上的櫻花一樣。

break〔brek〕v. 破壞

6. (**A**) 依句意為過去式，選 (A) *refused*「拒絕」。

7. (**B**) 東京「捐贈」三千棵櫻桃樹給華盛頓特區，選 (B) *donate*〔'donet〕
v. 捐贈。而 (A) devote〔dɪ'vot〕*v.* 使致力於，(C) owe〔o〕*v.* 欠，
(D) dedicate〔'dɛdə,ket〕*v.* 使致力於；奉獻（給神），均不合句意。

8. (**A**) 伊麗莎「很高興」，選 (A) *delighted*〔dɪ'laɪtɪd〕*adj.*（人）覺得高興
的。而 (B) delightful〔dɪ'laɪtfəl〕*adj.* 令人高興的，(C) pleasing
〔'plizɪŋ〕*adj.* 令人高興的，(D) pleasant〔'plɛzn̩t〕*adj.* 令人愉快的，
都修飾事物，用法與句意均不合。

9. (**D**) (A) health resort 療養勝地
    resort〔rɪ'zɔrt〕*n.* 渡假勝地；休養地
  (B) historic sites 歷史遺跡   site〔saɪt〕*n.* 地點；遺跡
  (C) amusement park 遊樂場
  (D) *tourist attraction* 觀光名勝

10. (**B**) 空格本應填 are one of the most famous tourist attractions，
但為避免重覆前面提過的名詞片語，故只保留 be 動詞 *are*，選 (B)。

TEST 9

Read the following passage, and choose the best answer for each blank.

Reading is the means ___1___ we obtain new ideas and concepts, and ___2___ our intellectual horizons. People who stop reading will stagnate intellectually. They will fall quickly behind the rest of the world and ___3___ with life and solve problems. All young people ___4___ in life should try to cultivate a love of books and the ability to read efficiently. Teachers and parents have a duty to provide guidance and develop among their children a permanent interest in reading. Yet young people themselves must ___5___ every day and try constantly to improve their reading skills.

1. A. in which
   B. by which
   C. for that
   D. by what

2. A. lower
   B. higher
   C. broaden
   D. rise

3. A. find hard to deal
   B. find hardly to cope
   C. find it hardly to deal
   D. find it hard to cope

4. A. ambitious for success
   B. with ambitious success
   C. with successful ambition
   D. are ambitious to succeed

5. A. get out of the habit of reading
   B. get rid of the habit to read
   C. get into the habit of reading
   D. get into the reader's habit

TEST 9 詳解

Reading is the means ⌐by **which** we obtain new ideas and con-
                              1

cepts, **and** *broaden* our intellectual horizons.⌐ People ⌐**who** stop read-
              2

ing⌐ will stagnate *intellectually*. They will fall *quickly* behind the rest

of the world **and** find it hard to cope with life **and** solve problems.
                           3

    藉由閱讀，我們可以獲得新的想法和概念，並且可以拓展知識的領域。停
止閱讀的人，在智能方面的發展就會停頓下來。他們很快就會跟不上時代，並
覺得生活難以應付，問題很難解決。

    means〔minz〕*n.* 方法；手段（單複數同形）
    obtain〔əb'ten〕*v.* 獲得   concept〔'kɑnsɛpt〕*n.* 概念
    horizons〔hə'raɪznz〕*n. pl.*（思想、知識的）範圍；領域
    stagnate〔'stægnet〕*v.* 停滯   *fall behind* 落後

1. (**B**) 依句意，應是「藉著閱讀這種方法」，故選 (B) *by which*。

2. (**C**) (A) lower〔'loɚ〕*v.* 降低
        (B) higher〔'haɪɚ〕*adj.* 較高的
        (C) *broaden*〔'brɔdn̩〕*v.* 增廣；拓展
        (D) rise〔raɪz〕*v.* 上升

3. (**D**) 依句意，選 (D) *find it hard to cope*。(A) 應改為 find it hard to
        deal，it 為虛受詞，代替後面的不定詞片語 to … problems。
        cope with 應付（= *deal with*）

All young people *ambitious for success* *in life* should try to cultivate
4

a love *of books* **and** the ability *to read efficiently.* Teachers and

parents have a duty *to provide guidance* **and** develop *among their*

children a permanent interest *in reading.* **Yet** young people them-

selves must get into the habit *of reading* every day **and** try
5

constantly to improve their reading skills.

凡是有抱負、想成功的年輕人，都應該培養對書本的喜好和閱讀的效率。老師及家長都有責任指導自己的孩子，培養他們對閱讀有永久的興趣。年輕人自己也必須養成每天閱讀的習慣，而且要不斷嘗試改進自己的閱讀技巧。

> cultivate (ˈkʌltəˌvet) *v.* 培養
> efficiently (əˈfɪʃəntlɪ, ɪ-) *adv.* 有效率地
> guidance (ˈgaɪdn̩s) *n.* 指導
> permanent (ˈpɝmənənt) *adj.* 永久的
> constantly (ˈkɑnstəntlɪ) *adv.* 不斷地；經常地
> improve (ɪmˈpruv) *v.* 改進

4. (**A**) All young people ambitious for success....
 ＝ All young people *who are* ambitious for success....
 ambitious (æmˈbɪʃəs) *adj.* 有抱負的

5. (**C**) 依句意，選 (C) *get into the habit of* + V-ing「養成～習慣」。
 而 (A) get out of「戒除」，(B) get rid of「擺脫」，則不合句意。

TEST 10

Read the following passage, and choose the best answer for each blank.

____1____ of the garbage we throw away can be used again.
____2____, we can reuse our own paper cups at home or in the
office. We can also use cardboard boxes and plastic bags to
put things in. ____3____, we should bring our own bags when we
____4____ shopping. In these ways we can reduce our garbage
and save a lot of space ____5____ for garbage.

Our ____6____ society has to change. We should ____7____ the
habit of bringing our own bags when ____8____. It may cause
some inconvenience, but it does help to keep the garbage
problem ____9____ more serious. If we all do our best to reduce
waste, we can make our environment cleaner, healthier and
____10____.

1. A. Many
   B. Much
   C. Few
   D. Little

2. A. In fact
   B. As a result
   C. For example
   D. At the same time

3. A. Most important of all
   B. In all
   C. All in all
   D. Most important

4. A. do
   B. go
   C. make
   D. deal

5. A. use
   B. using
   C. used
   D. to use

6. A. throw-away
   B. thrown-away
   C. away-throw
   D. throwing-away

7. A. go to
   B. get into
   C. build
   D. get

8. A. shop
   B. shopping
   C. we shopping
   D. shopped

9. A. growing
   B. to grow
   C. from growing
   D. by growing

10. A. beautiful
    B. more beautiful
    C. most beautiful
    D. less beautiful

TEST 10 詳解

Much of the garbage we throw away can be used again. For
　1

example, we can reuse our own paper cups at home or in the
　2

office. We can also use cardboard boxes and plastic bags to put

things in. Most important of all, we should bring our own bags
　　　　　　3

when we go shopping. In these ways we can reduce our garbage
　　4

and save a lot of space used for garbage.
　　　　　　　　　5

我們丟棄的垃圾，絕大部份都可再度使用。例如，我們可以將自己在家裏
或辦公室裏用過的紙杯回收再利用。也可以用厚紙箱和塑膠袋來裝東西。最重
要的是，去逛街購物時，應自備購物袋。這麼一來，就可以減少垃圾量，並且
省下許多原本會被垃圾所佔用的空間。

garbage (ˈgɑrbɪdʒ) n. 垃圾　　cardboard (ˈkɑrd,bord) n. 厚紙板
plastic (ˈplæstɪk) adj. 塑膠的

1. (**B**) garbage「垃圾」為不可數名詞，故須用 (B) much「很多」或
　　(D) little「很少」修飾。依句意，選 (B) **Much**。

2. (**C**) 依句意，選 (C) **For example**「例如」。而 (A) 事實上，(B) 因此，
　　(D) 同時，均不合句意。

3. (**A**) (A) ***most important of all*** 最重要的是

(B) in all 總計

(C) all in all 整個說來；大體而言

(D) most important 最重要的（不可單獨置於句首，以逗點隔開，故在此用法不合。）

4. (**B**) ***go shopping*** 去逛街購物

5. (**C**) 依句意，指被垃圾所佔用的空間，故空格應填過去分詞 ***used*** 表被動，選 (C)。原句是由… space which is used for garbage. 簡化而來。

Our throw-away society has to change. We should get into
        6   7

the habit *of bringing our own bags **when** shopping.* It may cause
                                      8

some inconvenience, ***but*** it does help to keep the garbage problem

from growing *more* serious. ***If** we all do our best to reduce waste,*
   9

we can make our environment cleaner, healthier ***and** more* beautiful.
                                             10

　　我們這個「用完即丟的」社會必須要改變了。購物時要養成自備購物袋的習慣。這可能會有些不方便，但這樣眞的有助於使垃圾問題不會變得更嚴重。如果我們都能盡力減少廢棄物，那麼就能使環境變得更乾淨、更健康，而且更加美麗。

      inconvenience〔͵ɪnkən'vinjəns〕*n.* 不方便

      reduce〔rɪ'djus〕*v.* 減少　　　waste〔west〕*n.* 廢棄物

      healthy〔'hɛlθɪ〕*adj.* 有益健康的

6. (**A**) *throw-away*〔'θroə,we〕*adj.* 用完即丟的

7. (**B**) *get into the habit of~* 養成~習慣

8. (**B**) 原句為…when we are shopping. 而副詞子句中，如果句意很明顯，可省略主詞與 be 動詞，故省略 we are 後，選 (B) *shopping*。

9. (**C**) 依句意，選 (C) keep the garbage problem *from growing* more serious「使垃圾問題不會變得更嚴重」。
keep ~ from + V-ing 使~免於…

10. (**B**) 由對等連接詞 and 可知，空格應選比較級形容詞，且依句意，使我們環境變得更乾淨、更健康，而且「更美麗」，故選 (B) *more beautiful*。

TEST 11

Read the following passage, and choose the best answer for each blank.

There was a nasty accident at Newton crossroads yesterday. A bus __1__, and some of the passengers were badly __2__. Several bystanders helped to pull people __3__ the wreckage and give them first aid __4__ help arrived. Soon the injured __5__ to the nearest hospital by ambulance, but there were so many that the casualty department had difficulty in treating them all.

1. A. turned down
   B. overturned
   C. took down
   D. overtook

2. A. pained
   B. wounded
   C. knocked down
   D. injured

3. A. to
   B. of
   C. in
   D. out of

4. A. until
   B. not until
   C. after
   D. that

5. A. took
   B. was taken
   C. were taken
   D. has taken

TEST 11 詳解

There was a nasty accident *at Newton crossroads yesterday.*

A bus overturned, *and* some *of the passengers* were *badly* injured.
　　　　　1　　　　　　　　　　　　　　　　　　　　　　　　　2

Several bystanders helped to pull people *out of the wreckage and*
　　　　　　　　　　　　　　　　　　　　　　　3

give them first aid *until help arrived.*
　　　　　　　　4

昨天在牛頓街的十字路口，發生了一件嚴重的車禍。有一輛公車翻覆了，部分乘客受到重傷。一些旁觀者，幫忙將乘客從公車殘骸中拉了出來，並在救援來到前對他們進行急救。

nasty ('næstɪ) *adj.* 嚴重的　　crossroads ('krɔs,rodz) *n. pl.* 十字路口
passenger ('pæsṇdʒɚ) *n.* 乘客　　bystander ('baɪ,stændɚ) *n.* 旁觀者
wreckage ('rɛkɪdʒ) *n.* 殘骸　　*first aid* 急救

1. (**B**) (A) turn down 關小聲
　　　　(B) *overturn* (,ovɚ'tɝn) *v.* 翻覆
　　　　(C) take down 拿下；拆毀 (建築物)
　　　　(D) overtake (,ovɚ'tek) *v.* 追上；超過

2. (**D**) 依句意，乘客在車禍中「受傷」，故選 (D) *injure* ('ɪndʒɚ) *v.* 傷害。
　　be injured 受傷　　而 (A) pain (pen) *n. v.* 疼痛，但無 be pained
　　的用法；(B) wound (wund) *n. v.* 傷害，be wounded 亦指「受傷」，
　　但通常指的是在戰爭中「受傷」，或指在感情或自尊等較抽象的事物
　　上受傷；(C) knock down 「擊倒；撞倒」，均不合句意。

3. (**D**) 依句意，旁觀者幫忙將受傷的乘客「從公車殘骸中拉出」，故選 (D)
　　out of。

4. (**A**) 依句意，旁觀者在救援來到之「前」，「一直」在對受傷者進行急救，
　　　故選 (A) ***until***。在此 until「直到～」，即相當於 before「在～之前」。

Soon　the　injured　<u>were　taken</u>　to　the　nearest　hospital　by　ambulance,
　　　　　　　　　　　　　　5

but　there　were　so　many　***that***　the　casualty　department　had　difficulty

in　treating　them　all.

不久之後，所有受傷的人，就被救護車載往最近的醫院，但受傷人數實在太多
了，以致於醫院的急診處，很難對所有傷者進行治療。

　　　ambulance〔ˈæmbjələns〕*n.* 救護車
　　　casualty〔ˈkæʒʊəltɪ〕*n.* 死傷的人
　　　have　difficulty　(***in***) + ***V-ing***　在～方面有困難

5. (**C**) 主詞 " the　injured " 在此指「所有受傷的人」，為複數名詞，故其
　　　動詞應用複數形，又人是被車載到醫院的，故須用被動語態，選 (C)
　　　were　taken。

TEST 12

Read the following passage, and choose the best answer for each blank.

Communist China today is ___1___ from the past ___2___ one important aspect. She is ___3___ longer isolated and ostracized ___4___ civilized international society. World opinion and the China policy of the major powers can and do ___5___ events in China. Anxious to project a good image, the better ___6___ and more worldly new leaders will be ___7___ to signals from ___8___, especially from those countries ___9___ are the ___10___ of investment and trade.

1. A. differ
   B. different
   C. difference
   D. differentiate

2. A. at
   B. on
   C. in
   D. to

3. A. no
   B. not
   C. any
   D. nor

4. A. by
   B. in
   C. at
   D. from

5. A. have
   B. influence
   C. cause
   D. make

6. A. educating
   B. educated
   C. educate
   D. to educate

7. A. able
   B. apt
   C. sensitive
   D. active

8. A. aboard
   B. abroad
   C. others
   D. outside

9. A. who
   B. they
   C. which
   D. those

10. A. resource
    B. information
    C. source
    D. origin

TEST 12 詳解

Communist China *today* is <u>different</u> from the past <u>*in* *one*</u>
                                    1   2

important aspect. She is <u>*no longer*</u> isolated and ostracized <u>*from*</u>
                                 3   4

civilized international society.

今日的中共在某個重要的方面不同於過去。她不再被孤立與被排斥於文明
的國際社會之外。

　　* 國家、交通工具的代名詞用 she 。

　　　　communist (ˈkɑmjʊˌnɪst) *adj.* 共產主義的
　　　　aspect (ˈæspɛkt) *n.* 方面　　isolate (ˈaɪslˌet) *v.* 使孤立；使隔離
　　　　ostracize (ˈɑstrəˌsaɪz) *v.* 排斥　　civilized (ˈsɪvlˌaɪzd) *adj.* 文明的

1. (**B**) **be different from** 不同於
　　(A) differ (ˈdɪfɚ) *v.* 不同　　(C) difference (ˈdɪfərəns) *n.* 不同
　　(D) differentiate (ˌdɪfəˈrɛnʃɪˌet) *v.* 辨別；區別

2. (**C**) **in ~ aspect** 在~方面　　aspect (ˈæspɛkt) *n.* 方面

3. (**A**) **no longer** 不再

4. (**D**) **be isolated from** 被~隔離
　　　　be ostracized from 被排斥於~之外

World opinion *and* the China policy <u>*of the major powers*</u> can *and*

do <u>influence</u> events *in China.* <u>*Anxious to project a good image,*</u>
          5

the *better* educated and *more* worldly new leaders will be <u>sensitive</u>
         6   7

to signals from abroad, especially from those countries which are
　　　　　　　　　　8　　　　　　　　　　　　　　　　　　　9

the source of investment and trade.
　　10

世界輿論和主要強權的中國政策，可以也眞的影響了在中國的事件。因爲急於要表現出良好的形象，受過較良好敎育，而且較世故的新領袖，對於來自國外的表示十分敏感，尤其是那些提供投資與貿易來源的國家。

* Anxious to …是由 Because they are anxious to …簡化而來。
　「do ＋ 原形動詞」加強原形動詞的語氣，表「眞的～」。

power〔ˋpauɚ〕*n.* 強國　　anxious〔ˋæŋkʃəs〕*adj.* 急切的
project〔prəˋdʒɛkt〕*v.* 生動地表現　　worldly〔ˋwɝldlɪ〕*adj.* 世故的
signal〔ˋsɪgnḷ〕*n.* 信號；表示

5. (**B**) 依句意，選 (B) influence〔ˋɪnfluəns〕*v.* 影響。而 (A) 有，(C) cause〔kɔz〕*v.* 造成。(D) 製造，均不合句意。

6. (**B**) well-educated「受過良好敎育的」，其比較級是 better-***educated***。

7. (**C**) ***be sensitive to ～*** 對～敏感　　sensitive〔ˋsɛnsətɪv〕*adj.* 敏感的
(A) be able to V. 能夠
(C) be apt to V. 易於；傾向於
(D) active〔ˋæktɪv〕*adj.* 活躍的

8. (**B**) 依句意，選 (B) ***from abroad***「來自國外」。
而 (A) aboard〔əˋbord〕*adv.* 在船上；在飛機上，(C) 其他人，
(D) outside〔ˋautˋsaɪd〕*n.* 外面，均不合句意。

9. (**C**) 空格應填一關係代名詞，代替先行詞 countries，故選 (C) ***which***。
而 (A) who 只能代替人，故不合。

10. (**C**) 依句意，選 (C) ***source***〔sors〕*n.* 來源。
(A) resource〔rɪˋsors〕*n.* 資源
(B) information〔ˏɪnfɚˋmeʃən〕*n.* 消息
(D) origin〔ˋɔrədʒɪn〕*n.* 起源

TEST 13

Read the following passage, and choose the best answer for each blank.

___1___ general, it is very important to know what types of books we should read. ___2___ the whole, we should read good literature ___3___ books of a professional knowledge. ___4___ should give the mind a stimulus for ideas. ___5___ a popular novel can give us pleasure, it should not be the main part of our literary books. ___6___, the mind will be limited. As you know, in reading serious writings, we should keep notes and think more ___7___ the lines; while reading popular novels or magazines, all we have to do is read for fun. We should also make sure that we have a quiet, ___8___ place to read in, and ___9___ we position the reading materials ___10___ least twelve inches from the eyes to protect our eyesight.

1. A. By
   B. In
   C. For
   D. To

2. A. On
   B. In
   C. As
   D. By

3. A. as many as
   B. as well as
   C. as long as
   D. as soon as

4. A. Which
   B. This
   C. They
   D. What

5. A. Although
    B. Unless
    C. Because
    D. Since

6. A. Accordingly
    B. Therefore
    C. Similarly
    D. Otherwise

7. A. with
    B. beyond
    C. between
    D. in

8. A. good-lighting
    B. good-lighted
    C. well-lighting
    D. well-lighted

9. A. that
    B. if
    C. which
    D. when

10. A. by
    B. at
    C. with
    D. from

TEST 13 詳解

In general, it is *very* important to know *what* types of books
1

we should read. *On* the whole, we should read good literature
2

as well as books *of a professional knowledge.* They should give
3   4

the mind a stimulus *for ideas.*

一般說來，知道自己該讀哪種類型的書，是非常重要的。大體而言，我們應該閱讀一些優秀的文學作品，以及與專業知識有關的書。這些書可以激發人們的想法。

type〔taɪp〕*n.* 類型　　literature〔'lɪtərətʃɚ〕*n.* 文學作品
professional〔prə'fɛʃənḷ〕*adj.* 專業的
give with 給予；提供　　stimulus〔'stɪmjələs〕*n.* 刺激；激勵

1. (**B**) *in general* 一般說來（= *generally speaking* ）

2. (**A**) *on the whole* 大體而言
　(C) as a whole 整個看來

3. (**B**) 以句意，選 (B) *as well as*「以及」。而 (A) as many as「多達」，
　(C) as long as「只要」，(D) as soon as「一…就～」，均不合句意。

4. (**C**) 依句意，「這些書」應該要能激發人們的想法，故代名詞用 *They*，選 (C)。

__Although__ a popular novel can give us pleasure, it should not be
　　5

the main part *of our literary books.* *Otherwise*, the mind will be
　　　　　　　　　　　　　　　　　　　　　6

limited. *As you know,* *in reading serious writings,* we should keep

notes *__and__* think *more* *between* the lines; *__while__* reading popular
　　　　　　　　　　　　　　　7

novels or magazines, all *we have to do* is read *for fun.*

雖然暢銷小說能帶給我們快樂，但卻不該讓它成爲我們文學性書籍的主體，否
則，會使我們的心智發展受到限制。大家都知道，在閱讀嚴肅的作品時，我們
應該要作筆記，並且要更注意其言外之意；在閱讀暢銷小說及雜誌時，我們所
必須做的，就純粹只是爲了樂趣而讀。

　　writing〔'raɪtɪŋ〕*n.* 著作；作品　　note〔not〕*n.* 筆記
　　__for fun__ 爲了樂趣

5. (**A**) 依句意，選 (A) *__Although__* 「雖然」。而 (B) 除非，(C) 因爲，(D) 既
　　　　然，均不合句意。

6. (**D**) 依句意，選 (D) *__Otherwise__* 「否則」。而 (A) accordingly〔ə'kɔrdɪŋlɪ〕
　　　　adv. 因此，(B) 因此，(C) similarly〔'sɪmələˑlɪ〕*adv.* 同樣地，則不合
　　　　句意。

7. (**C**) think *__between__* the lines 思考言外之意
　　　　read between the lines 領會言外之意

We should *also* make sure *that* we have a quiet, <u>well-lighted</u> place
                                                              10

to read in, **and** <u>**that**</u> we position the reading materials <u>at</u> least
                    9   **10**

twelve inches from the eyes to protect our eyesight.

我們也應該要確定,要有個安靜、光線良好的地方讀書,而且閱讀的資料,必須放在離眼睛至少十二英吋的地方,以保護我們的視力。

    position〔pə'zɪʃən〕*v.* 放置   eyesight〔'aɪ,saɪt〕*n.* 視力

8. (**D**) 依句意,選 (D) *well-lighted*「照明良好的」。
    light〔laɪt〕*v.* 照明;照亮

9. (**A**) 對等連接詞 and 連接兩個由 that 引導的名詞子句,作 believe 的受詞。

10. (**B**) *at least* 至少

TEST 14

Read the following passage, and choose the best answer for each blank.

___1___ four million Americans in the union of 13 states. Today, we are 60 times ___2___ in a union of 50 states. We have lighted the world with our inventions, ___3___ of our fellow citizens of the world wherever they cried out for help, journeyed to the moon and safely returned. So much has changed. And yet, here again we stand, together as centuries ago. And, once again, an American president freely chosen by a sovereign people ___4___ prescribed by the Constitution that guides us still. This alone is a cause for rejoicing, ___5___, there is more.

1. A. It had
   B. It were
   C. There were
   D. There had

2. A. again
   B. as much
   C. as many
   D. more

3. A. gone to the aid
   B. having helped
   C. following the footprints
   D. reached the extent

4. A. to abide by the promise
   B. has taken the oath
   C. keeping his words
   D. came to the understanding

5. A. which
   B. but
   C. unless
   D. where

TEST 14 詳解

There were four million Americans *in the union of 13 states.*
    1

Today, we are 60 times *as many in a union of 50 states.* We have
            2

lighted the world *with our inventions,* gone to the aid *of our fellow*
                        3

citizens of the world wherever they cried out for help, journeyed to

the moon *and safely* returned. *So* much has changed.

　　以前美國由十三州形成的聯邦，人口是四百萬。今天由五十個州形成的聯邦，人口是以前的六十倍。我們藉由自己的創造發明照亮了世界，我們幫助在世界上任何地方呼救的同胞，我們登陸月球並且安然返回。改變的地方實在太多了。

　　　union〔'junjən〕 *n.* 聯邦　　state〔stet〕 *n.* 州　　light〔laɪt〕 *v.* 照亮
　　　fellow citizen 同胞　　journey〔'dʒʒnɪ〕 *v.* 旅行

1. (**C**) 表示「有；存在」，要用 there be 表達，依句意爲過去式，且後接複數名詞，故選 (C) *There were*。

2. (**C**) *as many (Americans)* = *so many (Americans)*
    = *the same number of (Americans)*

3. (**A**) 空格本應填 have gone to the aid，但 have 前面已出現過，故予以省略。　　aid〔ed〕 *n.* 幫助　　*go to the aid of* ~ 去幫助~

And yet, here again we stand, *together as centuries ago.* ***And,*** *once*

again, an American president *freely chosen by a sovereign people*

has taken the oath *prescribed by the Constitution **that** guides us still.*
　　　　　　4

This *alone* is a cause *for rejoicing,* ***but,*** there is more.
　　　　　　　　　　　　　5

然而，和幾百年前一樣，我們又一起站在這裏。而且，又再一次地，由一群優
秀人民自由選舉產生的總統，也根據憲法的指示做了宣誓，這部憲法至今仍引
導著我們。光是這一點就值得我們歡欣鼓舞，何況還不止這些呢。

century〔'sɛntʃərɪ〕*n.* 世紀；一百年
sovereign〔'savrɪn〕*adj.* 卓越的　　prescribe〔prɪ'skraɪb〕*v.* 規定
constitution〔,kanstə'tjuʃən〕*n.* 憲法　　guide〔gaɪd〕*v.* 引導
cause〔kɔz〕*n.* 原因；理由　　rejoice〔rɪ'dʒɔɪs〕*v.* 欣喜；高興

4. (**B**) 本句的主詞是 president，空格中應填入主要動詞，而 (A) 爲不定詞，
　　　(C) 爲現在分詞，均不合。(D) 與句意不合，故選 (B)。
　　　(A) abide by 遵守
　　　(B) ***take the oath*** 宣誓　　oath〔oθ〕*n.* 宣誓
　　　(C) keep one's word 遵守諾言
　　　(D) come to the understanding 了解

5. (**B**) 空格應填一連接詞，連接前後二句，表「但是」，故選 (B) ***but***。
　　　(C) unless「除非」，也是連接詞，但其後不可加逗點，且句意也不合。

TEST 15

Read the following passage, and choose the best answer for each blank.

You are married and you flip a coin to see whether it will be you or your husband who gets pregnant. It sounds ___1___, but at least one expert thinks it could happen.

Lord Winston, a ___2___ expert in Britain, has said that ___3___ modern medical technology, doctors could ___4___ an embryo into a man's abdomen, let him carry it for nine months, and then ___5___ it by Caesarean section.

It would, of course, be dangerous, and many people would be ___6___ the idea. And among other problems: babies would ___7___ the terms *Mommy* and *Daddy*. Also, in emergencies, people wouldn't know whether ___8___ "Women and children first" or "Men and children first."

Fantastic ___9___ it is, it appears to be a technological advance the world is not ___10___.

    1. A. possible   2. A. fertility
        B. likely   B. nutrition
        C. impossible   C. ecology
        D. practicable   D. conservation

3. A. in
   B. for
   C. without
   D. with

4. A. transfuse
   B. implant
   C. instill
   D. import

5. A. deliver
   B. labor
   C. bear
   D. breed

6. A. oppose
   B. object
   C. against
   D. versus

7. A. compare
   B. mix
   C. confuse
   D. distinguish

8. A. yell
   B. to yell
   C. yelling
   D. should they

9. A. as
   B. although
   C. ever
   D. since

10. A. ready
    B. ready to
    C. ready for
    D. prepare for

TEST 15 詳解

You are married *and* you flip a coin to see *whether* it will be you or your husband *who* gets pregnant. It sounds impossible,
1
but at least one expert thinks *it could happen.*

　　妳結婚後，可以丟銅板來決定，是妳或妳的丈夫要懷孕。這聽來似乎不可能，但至少有位專家認為這可能會發生。

> flip〔flɪp〕*v.* 輕拋　　*flip a coin* 丟銅板
> pregnant〔'prɛgnənt〕*adj.* 懷孕的

1. (**C**) 依句意，選 (C) *impossible*「不可能的」。而 (A) 可能的，(B) 可能的，(D) practicable〔'præktɪkəbl〕*adj.* 可行的，均不合句意。

Lord Winston, *a fertility* expert in Britain, has said *that* with
2   3
modern medical technology, doctors could implant an embryo *into*
4
a man's abdomen, let him carry it *for nine months,* **and** then
deliver it *by Caesarean section.*
5

　　生育專家溫斯頓勛爵指出，利用現代醫療技術，醫生可以將胚胎植入男人的肚子裏，讓男人懷胎九個月，然後再剖腹，將小孩生出來。

> Lord〔lɔrd〕*n.* …勛爵〔對公爵（Duke）以外之貴族的尊稱〕
> embryo〔'ɛmbrɪ,o〕*n.* 胚胎　　abdomen〔'æbdəmən〕*n.* 腹部
> Caesarean section〔sɪ'zɛrɪən,sɛkʃən〕*n.* 剖腹生產手術
> （= *Caesarean operation*）
> 〔凱撒大帝（Julius Caesar）出生時，據說他母親不得不接受剖腹生產的方式，因此這種手術便以他的名字命名。〕

2. (**A**) 依句意，選 (A) ***fertility*** 〔 fə'tɪlətɪ 〕*n.* 生產力；繁殖力。
而 (B) nutrition 〔 nju'trɪʃən 〕*n.* 營養，(C) ecology 〔 ɪ'kɑlədʒɪ 〕*n.* 生態學，(D) conservation 〔ˌkɑnsə'veʃən 〕*n.* 保存；保育，均不合句意。

3. (**D**) 只要「用」現代的醫療技術，醫生可以將胚胎植入男人的肚子裏，故選 (D) ***with*** 。

4. (**B**) 依句意，選 (B) ***implant*** 〔 ɪm'plænt 〕*v.* 移植。
而 (A) transfuse 〔 træns'fjuz 〕*v.* 輸（血），(C) instill 〔 ɪn'stɪl 〕*v.* 灌輸，(D) import 〔 ɪm'pɔrt 〕*v.* 輸入，則不合句意。

5. (**A**) 將胚胎發育而成的嬰兒「出生來」，選 (A) ***deliver*** 〔 dɪ'lɪvə 〕*v.* 生（小孩）。而 (B) labor 〔'lebə 〕*n.* 生產的痛苦；陣痛，(C) bear 〔 bɛr 〕*v.* 生，(D) breed 〔 brid 〕*v.* 養育，用法與句意均不合。

It would, *of course*, be dangerous, ***and*** many people would

be <u>against</u> the idea. ***And*** among other problems: babies would
6

<u>confuse</u> the terms *Mommy* and *Daddy*. Also, *in emergencies*, people
7

wouldn't know ***whether <u>to yell</u>*** "*Women and children first*" ***or***
8

"*Men and children first*."

　　這當然是有危險性的，而且會有很多人反對這種想法。而其中最棘手的問題是：嬰兒會覺得「媽咪」和「爹地」這兩個名詞十分混淆。而且，在緊急情況中，人們會不知道是該大聲說：「婦女和小孩優先」還是「男士和小孩優先」。

> ***among other things*** 除了別的東西之外；尤其
> ***among other problems*** 除了別的問題之外；尤其
> term 〔 tɝm 〕*n.* 名詞；用語
> emergency 〔 ɪ'mɝdʒənsɪ 〕*n.* 緊急情況

6. (**C**) 表「反對」的說法：***be against***，故選 (C)。
　　　　　　　　　　　　= *oppose*
　　　　　　　　　　　　= *be opposed to*
　　　　　　　　　　　　= *object to*
　　　　　(D) versus〔ˈvɝsəs〕*prep.*（訴訟、比賽等）…對～（略作 vs.）

7. (**C**) 依句意，將「媽咪」和「爹地」這兩個名詞弄混，選 (C) ***confuse***
　　　　　〔kənˈfjuz〕*v.* 混淆；搞錯。而 (A) compare〔kəmˈpɛr〕*v.* 比較，
　　　　　(B) mix〔mɪks〕*v.* 混合，(D) distinguish〔dɪˈstɪŋgwɪʃ〕*v.* 區別，
　　　　　均不合句意。

8. (**B**) 「whether + to V.」表「是否應該～」，故選 (B) ***to yell***。
　　　　　yell〔jɛl〕*v.* 呼喊

*Fantastic **as** it is*, it appears to be a technological advance
　　　　　　　9

the world is not ready for.
　　　　　　　10

　　雖然這是件很棒的事，但這種先進的科技，世人似乎尚未做好心理準備能
夠來接受它。

　　　　fantastic〔fænˈtæstɪk〕*adj.* 了不起的；太棒了
　　　　technological〔͵tɛknəˈlɑdʒɪkḷ〕*adj.* 科技的
　　　　advance〔ədˈvæns〕*n.* 進步　　***the world*** 世人

9. (**A**) 原句為：Though it is fantastic…，將形容詞 fantastic 移至句
　　　　　首，though 可用 ***as*** 代替，仍表「雖然」。其用法為：

　　　形容詞 / 副詞　　　　　　　　though
　　　分詞 / (不含冠詞之) 名詞　　＋　as　　＋ S. + V.…「雖然～」

　　　　　但 although 不可置於句中，故不選。

10. (**C**) ***be ready for*** 為～做好準備（ = ***be prepared for*** ）。而 (B) be
　　　　　ready to 須加原形動詞，在此用法不合。

TEST 16

Read the following passage, and choose the best answer for each blank.

A tornado is a fierce and ___1___ whirling windstorm. It may whirl clockwise or counterclockwise. When a tornado occurs over the ocean, it is called a waterspout. Tornadoes occur most often during the spring and summer ___2___ during these seasons warm air is most ___3___ to meet fast-moving cold fronts. In the United States, tornadoes do more damage ___4___ people than any other kind of windstorm. They cause the death of many people and do damage which ___5___ millions of dollars.

1. A. calm
   B. violent
   C. shallow
   D. flat

2. A. but
   B. because
   C. though
   D. that

3. A. likely
   B. liked
   C. liking
   D. likewise

4. A. on
   B. to
   C. for
   D. at

5. A. brings in
   B. takes over
   C. adds up to
   D. searches for

TEST 16 詳解

A tornado is a fierce and <u>violent</u> whirling windstorm. It may
₁

whirl *clockwise or counterclockwise.* ***When*** *a tornado occurs over*

the ocean, it is called a waterspout. Tornadoes occur *most often*

during the spring and summer **because** *during these seasons warm*
₂

air is most likely to meet fast-moving cold fronts.
₃

龍捲風是一種猛烈而狂暴的旋風。它可以順時針或逆時針方向旋轉。當龍
捲風發生在海上時，便稱為海上龍捲風。龍捲風大多發生在春夏間，因為此時
暖空氣最有可能遇到快速移動的冷鋒。

> tornado〔tɔr'nedo〕*n.* 龍捲風　　fierce〔fɪrs〕*adj.* 猛烈的
> whirl〔hwɜl〕*v.* 旋轉　　windstorm〔'wɪnd,stɔrm〕*n.* 狂風
> clockwise〔'klɑk,waɪz〕*adv.* 順時針方向地
> counterclockwise〔,kaʊntɚ'klɑk,waɪz〕*adv.* 逆時針方向地
> waterspout〔'wɑtɚ,spaʊt〕*n.* 海上龍捲風　　***cold front*** 冷鋒

1. (**B**) (A) calm〔kɑm〕*adj.* 平靜的　　(B) ***violent***〔'vaɪələnt〕*adj.* 猛烈的
　　　　(C) shallow〔'ʃælo〕*adj.* 淺的　　(D) flat〔flæt〕*adj.* 平坦的

2. (**B**) because … fronts 是副詞子句，修飾 occur，表原因。

3. (**A**) ***be likely to*** 可能
　　　　(C) liking〔'laɪkɪŋ〕*n.* 愛好
　　　　(D) likewise〔'laɪk,waɪz〕*adv.* 同樣地

In the United States, tornadoes do more damage to people *than*
4

any other kind of windstorm. They cause the death *of many people*

and do damage *which* adds up to millions of dollars.
5

在美國，龍捲風所造成的損害，比其他任何一種狂風都嚴重。龍捲風會使許多人死亡，且造成高達數百萬美元的損失。

4. (**B**) *do damage to* ~ 對~造成損害

5. (**C**) (A) bring in 使賺進（錢）
 (B) take over 接管
 (C) *add up to* 總計達
 (D) search for 尋找

TEST 17

Read the following passage, and choose the best answer for each blank.

The proverb that time is money ___1___ far short of the truth. Time is worth more than money ___2___ its wise employment more wisdom can be secured than money can purchase.

Reading is easy, and thinking is hard work, but ___3___ is useless without the other. The reading that ___4___ is the reading which, in making a man ___5___, stirs, and exercises and polishes the edge of his mind. The end of reading is not to possess knowledge ___6___ a man possesses dollars in his wallet, but to make knowledge a part of ourselves, ___7___ to turn knowledge into thought, as the food we eat is turned into the ___8___ and nerve-nourishing blood. It is to have a mind so stored and equipped that it shall be to each man his kingdom, ___9___ no one can deprive ___10___.

1. A. makes
   B. falls
   C. breaks
   D. cuts

2. A. because
   B. because of
   C. because by
   D. because of by

3. A. once
   B. the one
   C. another
   D. some

4. A. accounts
   B. counts
   C. amounts
   D. accustoms

5. A. thought
   B. thoughts
   C. thinks
   D. think

6. A. as
   B. so
   C. what
   D. that

7. A. what is
   B. which is
   C. it is
   D. that is

8. A. life-giving
   B. life-given
   C. live-giving
   D. live-given

9. A. of which
   B. of whom
   C. for which
   D. for whom

10. A. us
    B. you
    C. him
    D. them

TEST 17 詳解

The proverb *that* time is money falls *far* short of the truth.
1

Time is worth more *than* money *because* *by* its wise employment
2

more wisdom can be secured *than* money can purchase.

「時間就是金錢」這句諺語，與事實相差甚遠。時間比金錢有價值，因爲藉著明智地運用時間，所獲得的智慧比金錢能夠買到的多。

proverb〔ˋprɑvɝb〕*n.* 諺語   employment〔ɪmˋplɔɪmənt〕*n.* 運用
secure〔sɪˋkjʊr〕*v.* 獲得   purchase〔ˋpɝtʃəs〕*v.* 購買

1. (**B**) *fall short of* 未達到；不符合

2. (**C**) 空格後爲一完整子句，故此處需要連接詞 because，且依句意，「藉著明智地運用時間」爲一副詞片語，亦需介系詞 by，故選 (C)。

Reading is easy, *and* thinking is hard work, *but* the one is
3

useless *without the other*. The reading *that* counts is the reading
4

which, *in making a man think*, stirs, *and* exercises *and* polishes the
5

edge of his mind.

閱讀容易思考難，但若不思考，閱讀也毫無用處。眞正重要的閱讀，在於讓人思考，能夠激發、運用並使人的頭腦更加敏銳。

stir〔stɝ〕v. 激發　　polish〔'pɑlɪʃ〕v. 使完美；改進
edge〔ɛdʒ〕n. 敏銳

3. (**B**) *the one … the other* ~　前者…後者~
　　(= *the former … the latter* ~)

4. (**B**) 依句意，眞正「重要」的閱讀，動詞用 *count*〔kaʊnt〕v. 重要，選 (B)。
　　而 (A) account〔ə'kaʊnt〕v. 說明，(C) amount〔ə'maʊnt〕v. 總計，
　　(D) accustom〔ə'kʌstəm〕v. 使習慣，均不合句意。

5. (**D**) make 爲使役動詞，接受詞後須接原形動詞，故選 (D) *think*。

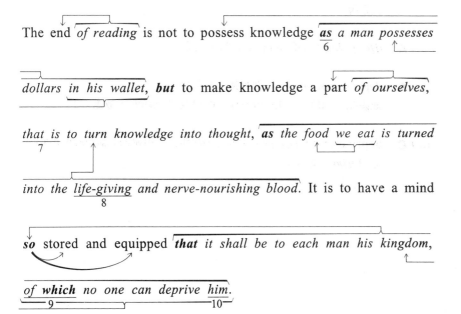

The end *of reading* is not to possess knowledge *as a man possesses*
　　　　　　　　　　　　　　　　　　　　　　　　　6

dollars in his wallet, ***but*** to make knowledge a part *of ourselves,*

that is to turn knowledge into thought, ***as*** *the food we eat is turned*
　7

into the life-giving and nerve-nourishing blood. It is to have a mind
　　　　　　　　　　　　　8

so stored and equipped ***that*** *it shall be to each man his kingdom,*

of ***which*** *no one can deprive him.*
　　　9　　　　　　　　　10

閱讀的目的，不在於使人像皮夾裏擁有金錢般擁有知識，而在於讓知識成為我們的一部分，也就是將知識變成思想，正如我們所吃的食物，變成賦予生命、滋養神經的血液一樣。閱讀的目的是要將人的心靈儲備起來，使其更豐富，以成為沒有人能夠剝奪的，屬於每個人自己的領域。

      end〔ɛnd〕*n.* 目的   possess〔pə'zɛs〕*v.* 擁有

      wallet〔'wɑlɪt〕*n.* 皮夾   nerve〔nɝv〕*n.* 神經

      nourish〔'nɝʃ〕*v.* 滋養   store〔stor〕*v.* 儲存

      equip〔ɪ'kwɪp〕*v.* 裝備；使具有   kingdom〔'kɪŋdəm〕*n.* 王國；領域

      deprive〔dɪ'praɪv〕*v.* 剝奪

6. (**A**) 依句意，「像皮夾裏擁有金錢一樣擁有知識」，故選 (A) *as*「像～一樣」。

7. (**D**) 空格後的句子，是針對空格前的句子加以說明，故選 (D) *that is*「也就是說」。

8. (**A**) *life-giving*〔'laɪf‚gɪvɪŋ〕*adj.* 賦予生命的

9. (**A**) *deprive sb. of sth.* 剝奪某人的某物

    此處先行詞為 his kingdom，關代須用 *which*，故選 (A)。

10. (**C**) deprive 之後的代名詞，代替句子前段已出現過的名詞 each man，故用 *him*，選 (C)。

TEST 18

Read the following passage, and choose the best answer for each blank.

The term university was first used over 750 years ago in Paris to __1__ to a corporation formed jointly by masters and students to better protect their own __2__ interests. As a result, master and student were __3__ an equal basis in the beginning. In Bologna the students actually founded their own university, retaining for a while the right to __4__ and fire their masters, that is, their teachers. They were even __5__ to fire professors who dared to continue their lectures one minute past the bell.

1. A. infer
   B. confer
   C. point
   D. refer

2. A. mutual
   B. eternal
   C. temporary
   D. vocational

3. A. in
   B. on
   C. with
   D. at

4. A. rent
   B. hire
   C. purchase
   D. acquire

5. A. familiar
   B. accustomed
   C. known
   D. used

TEST 18 詳解

The term *university* was *first* used *over 750 years ago* *in Paris*

to refer to a corporation *formed jointly by masters and students to*
$\underline{}$
1

better protect their own <u>mutual</u> *interests.* *As a result*, master and
2

student were <u>on</u> an equal basis *in the beginning.*
3

大學這個名詞，在七百五十多年前的巴黎首次被使用，當時是指老師及學生共同組成的校務委員會，以進一步保護他們共同的利益。因此，一開始老師和學生是處在平等的基礎上。

term (tɜm) *n.* 名詞；術語
corporation (ˌkɔrpəˈreʃən) *n.* (大學的) 校務委員會
form (fɔrm) *v.* 形成　　jointly (ˈdʒɔɪntlɪ) *adv.* 共同地
master (ˈmæstɚ, ˈmɑs-) *n.* 教師　　equal (ˈikwəl) *adj.* 平等的

1. (**D**) 依句意，選 (D) ***refer to*** 「是指」。而 (A) infer (ɪnˈfɜ) *v.* 推論，
   (B) confer (kənˈfɜ) *v.* 授與；商談，(C) point (pɔɪnt) *v.* 指出，均
   不合句意。

2. (**A**) 依句意，大學是由老師及學生共同組成，以進一步保護彼此「共同
   的」利益，故選 (A) ***mutual*** (ˈmjutʃʊəl) *adj.* 共同的。而 (B) eternal
   (ɪˈtɜnḷ) *adj.* 永恒的，(C) temporary (ˈtɛmpəˌrɛrɪ) *adj.* 暫時的，
   (D) vocational (voˈkeʃənḷ) *adj.* 職業的，均不合句意。

3. (**B**) ***on ~ basis*** 在~的基礎上

In Bologna the students *actually* founded their own university,

retaining for a while the right to <u>hire</u> and *fire their masters, that*
　　　　　　　　　　　　　4

is, their teachers. They were *even* <u>known</u> to fire professors *who*
　　　　　　　　　　　　　　　　5

dared to continue their lectures one minute past the bell.

在波隆那，學生眞的建立起自己的大學，而且曾有一陣子，他們有權利雇用和開除他們的授業人，也就是老師。大家都知道，他們甚至曾開除，在下課鈴響一分鐘後，還敢繼續講課的敎授。

Bologna〔bə'lonjə〕*n.* 波隆那（義大利北部的城市）
found〔faʊnd〕*v.* 建立　　retain〔rɪ'ten〕*v.* 保有
for a while 一陣子　　fire〔faɪr〕*v.* 開除　　*that is* 也就是
dare to + V. 敢～　　lecture〔'lɛktʃə〕*n.* 講課

4. (**B**)　(A) rent〔rɛnt〕*v.* 租　　　　　(B) *hire*〔haɪr〕*v.* 雇用
　　　　　　(C) purchase〔'pɜtʃəs〕*v.* 購買　(D) acquire〔ə'kwaɪr〕*v.* 獲得

5. (**C**)　依句意，選 (C) *known*。原句相當於 It was even *known* that
　　　　　they fired professors …。而 (A) be familiar to ~「爲～所熟悉」，
　　　　　(B) be accustomed to ~ = (D) be used to ~「習慣於～」，後
　　　　　須接動名詞，在此用法不合。

TEST 19

Read the following passage, and choose the best answer for each blank.

You would think that dying your hair would be pretty safe. Sure, you might ___1___ looking like Ronald McDonald, but this will only damage your ___2___, not your health.

Recent studies in the United States, ___3___, have suggested that there might be a link between ___4___ and some skin problems. Unfortunately, hair dyes ___5___ coal tar cannot be controlled by the U.S. Food and Drug Administration, ___6___ is responsible for checking other cosmetics.

A simple test can probably ___7___ the safety of a hair dye. Dab a little of the dye behind your ear and ___8___ it there for two days. If you don't notice any burning or itching, then you should be OK.

Of course, you still have to choose the right ___9___, and there's no easy test for that. If you make a mistake, you may spend a month ___10___ like Ronald McDonald!

1. A. make up
   B. call up
   C. end up
   D. put up

2. A. eyesight
   B. looks
   C. appetite
   D. taste

3. A. however
   B. instead
   C. therefore
   D. thus

4. A. hair cutting
   B. hair styles
   C. hairdos
   D. hair coloring

5. A. made from
   B. made of
   C. made into
   D. made by

6. A. it
   B. which
   C. and which
   D. that

7. A. ensure
   B. endanger
   C. guard
   D. guaranty

8. A. remain
   B. contain
   C. leave
   D. stay

9. A. beautician
   B. brand
   C. style
   D. color

10. A. look
    B. to look
    C. looking
    D. being looked

TEST 19 詳解

You would think *that dying your hair would be pretty safe.*
Sure, you might <u>end up</u> looking like Ronald McDonald, *but* this
                   1
will *only* damage your <u>looks</u>, not your health.
                            2

你會以爲染髮是很安全的。當然，最後你可能會看起來像麥當勞叔叔，但
這只會損害你的外表，而非健康。

> dye〔daɪ〕*v.* 染料　　pretty〔ˈprɪtɪ〕*adv.* 非常地
> *Ronald McDonald* 麥當勞叔叔

1. (**C**) 依句意，選 (C) *end up*「結果（成爲）」。而 (A) make up「編造；
   化粧」，(B) call up「打電話給～」，(D) put up「舉起；張貼」，
   均不合句意。

2. (**B**) 只是「外表」受損，而非健康，選 (B) *looks*〔luks〕*n. pl.* 外表。
   而 (A) eyesight〔ˈaɪˌsaɪt〕*n.* 視力，(C) appetite〔ˈæpəˌtaɪt〕*n.* 食慾，
   (D) taste〔test〕*n.* 品味；愛好，則不合句意。

Recent studies *in the United States,* <u>however</u>, have suggested
                                             3
that there might be a link between <u>hair coloring</u> *and some skin*
                                          4
problems. Unfortunately, hair dyes <u>made from</u> coal tar cannot be
                                          5
controlled *by the U.S. Food and Drug Administration,* ***which*** is
                                                                      6
responsible for checking other cosmetics.

　　然而最近美國研究報告指出，染髮和某些皮膚問題可能有關。不幸的是，由煤焦油所製成的頭髮染料，並不受到美國食品藥物管理局的管制，該局是專門負責檢查其他種類的化粧品。

recent (´risṇt) *adj.* 最近的　　　link (lɪŋk) *n.* 關連
coal tar 煤焦油　　administration (əd͵mɪnə´streʃən) *n.* 行政機關
be responsible for 負責　　cosmetics (kɑz´mɛtɪks) *n. pl.* 化粧品

3. (**A**) 前後語氣有轉折，故選 (A) *however*「然而」。而 (B) instead「相反地；取而代之」，(C) 因此，(D) 因此，均不合句意。

4. (**D**) 依句意，選 (D) *hair coloring*「染髮」。color (´kʌlɚ) *v.* 將～染色 而 (A) hair cutting「剪髮」，(B) hair style「髮型」，(C) hairdo (´hɛr͵du) *n.* 髮型，均不合句意。

5. (**A**) 本句是由…hair dyes *which are made from* coal tar…簡化而來。而 (A) be made from「由～製成」(經過化學變化，原料看不出來)，(B) be made of「由～製成」(經過物理變化，看得出原料)，依句意，選 (A)。(C) be made into「被製成～ (產品)」，(D) be made by「由～ (人) 製造」，則用法不合。

6. (**B**) 空格應填一關代，引導補述用法的形容詞子句，補充說明先行詞 the U.S. Food and Drug Administration，故選 (B) *which*。因空格前有逗點，故 (D) that 不可選。

A simple test can *probably* ensure the safety *of a hair dye.*
　　　　　　　　　　　　　7

Dab a little of the dye *behind your ear **and** leave it there *for*
　　　　　　　　　　　　　　　　　　　　　 8

two days. *If you don't notice any burning or itching,* *then* you

should be OK.

有個簡單的測試，可以確定頭髮的染料是否安全。在耳後隨便塗上一點染料，讓它停留兩天。如果你沒有任何火熱或刺癢的感覺，那麼就沒問題了。

dab〔dæb〕v. 隨便塗上　　burning〔'bɜnɪŋ〕n. 燃燒
itching〔'ɪtʃɪŋ〕n. 刺癢

7. (**A**) 做簡單的測試，「確定」頭髮染料是否安全，故選 (A) ***ensure***〔ɪn'ʃʊr〕
v. 使確定。而 (B) endanger〔ɪn'dendʒɚ〕v. 使有危險，(C) guard
〔gɑrd〕v. 看守，(D) guaranty〔'gærəntɪ〕n. 保證書，均不合句意。

8. (**C**) 將染料「留」在那裏，選 (C) ***leave***〔liv〕vt. 留下；遺留。而 (A) remain
〔rɪ'men〕vi. 留下，爲不及物動詞，不可接受詞；(B) contain
〔kən'ten〕v. 包含，不合句意；(D) stay〔ste〕vi. 停留，不可接受
詞，用法不合。

Of course, you *still* have to choose the right color, ***and***
　　　　　　　　　　　　　　　　　　　　　　　9
there's no easy test for that. *If you make a mistake*, you may
spend a month looking like Ronald McDonald！
　　　　　　　10

當然，你還是得選擇正確的顏色，而這並不容易測試。如果你選錯顏色，那可能就得有一個月的時間看起來像麥當勞叔叔。

9. (**D**) 依句意，染髮要選對「顏色」，選 (D) ***color***〔'kʌlɚ〕n. 顏色。
而 (A) beautician〔bju'tɪʃən〕n. 美容師，(B) brand〔brænd〕n.
品牌，(C) style〔staɪl〕n. 風格，則不合句意。

10. (**C**) 「spend + 時間 + (in) + V-ing」表「度過～（時間）…」，且依
句意爲主動，故選 (C) ***looking***。

TEST 20

Read the following passage, and choose the best answer for each blank.

Grown-ups love figures. When you tell them that you have made a new friend, they never ask you any questions about essential matters. They never say to you, "___1___ does he look? What games does he love best?" ___2___, they demand, "How old is he? How many brothers has he? How much money does his father make?" Only from these figures ___3___ they have learned anything about him.

If you were to say to the grown-ups, "I saw a beautiful house ___4___ rosy brick, with tulips in the windows and doves on the roof," they would not be able to get any idea of that house at all. You would have to say to them, "I saw a house that cost $20,000." Then they would exclaim, "Oh, what a pretty house it is!"

They are like that. One must not hold it ___5___ them. Children should always show great patience toward grown-up people.

1. A. What
   B. What appearance
   C. How
   D. How difference

2. A. On the contrary
   B. On the other hand
   C. In addition
   D. Instead

3. A. they are sure
   B. are they really recognized
   C. do they think
   D. do they convince

4. A. made of
   B. which is made with
   C. made up of
   D. which covered with

5. A. with
   B. against
   C. for
   D. on

TEST 20 詳解

Grown-ups love figures. *When you tell them that you have made a new friend*, they *never* ask you any questions *about essential matters*. They *never* say to you, "How does he look? What games does he love *best*?" *Instead*, they demand, "How old is he? How many brothers has he? How much money does his father make?" *Only from these figures* do they think they have learned anything about him.

大人們很喜歡數字。當你告訴他們你交了新朋友時,他們絕不會問你一些重要的問題。他們絕不會問說:「他長得如何?他最喜歡玩什麼遊戲?」而是問說:「他今年幾歲?他有幾個兄弟?他爸爸賺多少錢?」大人們認為,唯有經由這些數字,他們才能對你的新朋友有所了解。

grown-up (ˈgronˌʌp) *n.* 成人;大人　　figure (ˈfɪgjɚ) *n.* 數字
essential (əˈsɛnʃəl) *adj.* 重要的;必要的
demand (dɪˈmænd) *v.* 查問;要求

1. (**C**) *How* does he look? 他長得怎麼樣?

2. (**D**) (A) 相反地　　(B) 另一方面　　(C) 此外　　(D) 代替地;改換

3. (**C**)「only + 副詞片語或子句」置於句首時,主要子句的助動詞或 be 動詞應放在主詞前,形成倒裝,故選 (C) *do they think*。而 (A) 須改為 are they sure,(B) 須改為 do they really recognize,(D) 須改為 are they convinced。

If you were to say to the grown-ups, "I saw a beautiful house

__made of__ *rosy brick,* with tulips in the windows **and** doves on the
4

__roof,__" they would not be able to get any idea *of that house* at all.

You would have to say to them, "I saw a house **that cost** $20,000."

Then they would exclaim, "Oh, what a pretty house it is!"

They are like that. One must not hold it <u>against</u> them.
5

Children should *always* show great patience *toward grown-up people.*

如果你對大人說：「我看見一棟漂亮的房子，是用玫瑰色磚頭砌成的，窗前有鬱金香，屋頂上有鴿子。」他們會對這房子毫無概念。你可能必須對他們說：「我看見一棟價值兩萬元的房子。」那麼他們就會大叫說：「噢，那是棟多麼美的房子啊！」

大人們就是這樣。我們不應該怪他們。小孩子對大人總是要很有耐心才行。

rosy ('rozɪ) *adj.* 玫瑰色的　　brick (brɪk) *n.* 磚頭
tulip ('tjuləp , 'tu- , -ɪp) *n.* 鬱金香　　dove (dʌv) *n.* 鴿子
exclaim (ɪk'sklem) *v.* 呼喊；驚叫　　grown-up ('gron,ʌp) *adj.* 成人的

4. (**A**) 依句意，房子是由磚頭「所建造而成」，故應選 (A) **made of**。
原句… a beautiful house made of …是由… a beautiful house *which is* made of …簡化而來。
be made of ~ 由（~材料）所製造
be made up of ~ 由（~要素）所組成
be covered with ~ 由~所覆蓋

5. (**B**) **hold** *sth.* **against** *sb.* 因某事而降低對某人的評價；因某事而對某人存有偏見

TEST 21

Read the following passage, and choose the best answer for each blank.

Cats are excellent hunters. Why? They have extremely __1__ senses. No touch is too __2__ for cats to feel. Even through thick fur, cats feel the slightest change __3__ temperature. Cats hear little noises as though they __4__ loud. No cat could miss the light movements of tiny mice feet on dry fall leaves.

Taste may be a cat's weakest sense. But its nose __5__. A cat __6__ sniffs food before eating. __7__ love pleasant smells. When cats go outside, they follow their noses.

A cat's eyes move __8__. Its whole head moves to keep track of a fly. Light affects a cat's eyes. The pupils of __9__ become thin lines in sunlight. At night they become wide and round. Cats see very well at night.

Cats do not have nine lives. But __10__ such sharp senses, do they need more than one?

1. A. strong
   B. real
   C. keen
   D. high

2. A. light
   B. heavy
   C. small
   D. big

3. A. from
   B. to
   C. on
   D. in

4. A. are
   B. were
   C. had been
   D. had had

5. A. helps
   B. shows
   C. does
   D. makes

6. A. rarely
   B. usually
   C. hardly
   D. scarcely

7. A. A cat
   B. The cat
   C. Cats
   D. The cats

8. A. joyfully
   B. socially
   C. partly
   D. slowly

9. A. the eye
   B. an eye
   C. eyes
   D. the eyes

10. A. with
    B. of
    C. under
    D. by

TEST 21 詳解

Cats are excellent hunters. Why? They have *extremely* keen
1

senses. No touch is *too* light for cats to feel. *Even through thick*
2

fur, cats feel the slightest change *in temperature*. Cats hear little
3

noises *as though they were loud*. No cat could miss the light
4

movements *of tiny mice feet on dry fall leaves*.

貓是很優秀的狩獵者。爲什麼？因爲他們有非常敏銳的感覺，再輕微的碰
觸，他們都感受得到。雖然是透過濃密的皮毛，他們仍能感覺到氣溫最細微的
變化。小小的聲音對貓來說是很大聲的，像是小老鼠踩在秋天乾枯落葉的輕微
動作，貓也都能注意到。

> excellent〔'ɛkslənt〕*adj.* 優秀的
> extremely〔ɪk'strimlɪ〕*adv.* 非常地　　fur〔fɝ〕*n.* 毛皮
> *as though* 就好像　　tiny〔'taɪnɪ〕*adj.* 微小的
> mice〔maɪs〕*n. pl.* 老鼠（單數是 mouse）　　fall〔fɔl〕*n.* 秋天

1. (**C**) 依句意，選 (C) *keen*〔kin〕*adj.* 敏銳的。

2. (**A**) 依句意，選 (A) *light*〔laɪt〕*adj.* 輕的。

3. (**D**) *change in* ~ 表「在某方面的改變」，故選 (D)。

4. (**B**) 依句意爲與現在事實相反之假設，be 動詞須用 were，故選 (B)。

Taste may be a cat's weakest sense. ***But*** its nose helps. A cat
5

usually sniffs food *before eating.* Cats love pleasant smells. ***When***
6　　　　　　　　　　　　　　　　　　7

cats go outside, they follow their noses.

　　味覺可能是貓最弱的感覺。但牠的鼻子卻能提供補救。貓通常在吃東西以
前都要先聞一聞。貓喜歡令其愉悅的味道。貓在外出時，都是靠鼻子的嗅覺行
動。

　　　sniff (snɪf) v. 嗅　　pleasant ('plɛznt) adj. 令人愉快的
　　　follow ('falo) v. 接受～的領導

5. (**A**) 依句意，選 (A) *helps*「有幫助」。

6. (**B**) 依句意，選 (B) ***usually***「通常」。而 (A) rarely ('rɛrlɪ) adv. 很少，
　　　(C) hardly「幾乎不」，(D) scarcely ('skɛrslɪ) adv. 幾乎不，均不合
　　　句意。

7. (**C**) 表「全體的貓」，可寫成 A cat, The cat, 或 Cats，由於動詞love
　　　爲複數動詞，故選 (C) ***Cats***。

A cat's eyes move *slowly.* Its whole head moves *to keep track*
8

of a fly. Light affects a cat's eyes. The pupils *of the eyes* become
9

thin lines *in sunlight. At night* they become wide and round. Cats

see *very well at night.*

貓的眼睛動得很慢，所以為了要追蹤一隻蒼蠅，牠的頭部必須整個移動。光線會對其眼睛產生影響。在陽光下，貓的眼睛的瞳孔會變成像細線一般。到了夜晚，卻又變得又圓又大。因此在晚上，貓的眼睛看得非常清楚。

> ***keep track of*** 跟蹤　　**fly** (flaɪ) *n.* 蒼蠅
> **pupil** (ˈpjupḷ) *n.* 瞳孔　　**thin** (θɪn) *adj.* 細的

8. (**D**) 依句意，貓的眼睛動得很「慢」，故選 (D) ***slowly*** 「緩慢地」。
而 (A) joyfully (ˈdʒɔɪfəlɪ) *adv.* 愉快地，(B) socially (ˈsoʃəlɪ) *adv.* 社交地，(C) 部分地，均不合句意。

9. (**D**) 由於 pupils 為複數，因此空格應填複數名詞，並加上定冠詞 the，故選 (D) ***the eyes***，在此指「貓的眼睛」。

Cats do not have nine lives. ***But with such sharp senses***, do they need more than one?
10

貓並沒有九條命，但是擁有如此敏銳的感官，牠們還需要更多條命嗎？

> **sharp** (ʃɑrp) *adj.* 敏銳的

10. (**A**) 介系詞 with 在此表「具有」，相當於 having。

TEST 22

Read the following passage, and choose the best answer for each blank.

My husband, a psychology professor, teaches a course in parenting and always emphasizes the importance of reinforcing good behavior ___1___ praise or a hug. Since I am a youth counselor, he invited me to ___2___ my experiences with his class. I was introduced to the students, and because I used my maiden name, they could not have known we were ___3___.

When I finished my talk, my husband surprised both me and the class. "Don't you think Ms. Street ___4___ a good job in her presentation? Shouldn't we reward her?" he asked.

I expected a polite round of applause, but instead, my normally reserved husband swept me into his arms and kissed me. "That, students, is reinforcement," he told the ___5___ onlookers. "Class dismissed."

1. A. in
   B. of
   C. with
   D. over

2. A. express
   B. tell
   C. show
   D. share

3. A. divorced
   B. engaged
   C. separated
   D. married

4. A. did
   B. made
   C. took
   D. present

5. A. interesting
   B. frightening
   C. contented
   D. stunned

TEST 22 詳解

My husband, *a psychology professor*, teaches a course *in parenting* **and** *always* emphasizes the importance *of reinforcing good behavior with praise* **or** *a hug.* ***Since*** *I am a youth counselor*, he invited me to share my experiences *with his class.* I was introduced to the students, ***and because*** *I used my maiden name*, they could not have known *we were married.*

　　我的丈夫是位心理學教授，教的是有關父母照顧小孩的課程，他常常強調，以讚美或擁抱，來獎勵好的行為，是很重要的。由於我是一位青少年諮商人員，所以他邀請我到他班上，和同學們分享我的經驗。他向學生介紹我，由於我使用的是本姓，所以大家都不知道我是他的妻子。

> psychology〔saɪ'kɑlədʒɪ〕*n.* 心理學　　professor〔prə'fɛsɚ〕*n.* 教授
> parenting〔'pɛrəntɪŋ〕*n.* 父母對小孩的照顧
> reinforce〔‚riɪn'fors〕*v.* 加強　　hug〔hʌg〕*n.* 擁抱
> counselor〔'kaʊnslɚ〕*n.* 顧問　　*maiden name*（已婚婦女的）本姓

1. (**C**) 依句意，「用」讚美和擁抱，來獎勵他們良好的行為，故選 (C) *with*。

2. (**D**) *share sth. with sb.* 與某人分享某物

3. (**D**) (A) divorced〔də'vorst , -'vɔrst〕*adj.* 離婚的
　　　　(B) engaged〔ɪn'gedʒd〕*adj.* 已訂婚的
　　　　(C) separated〔'sɛpə‚retɪd〕*adj.* 分開的；分居的
　　　　(D) *married*〔'mærɪd〕*adj.* 已結婚的

When I finished my talk, my husband surprised both me *and*

the class. "Don't you think *Ms. Street did a good job in her*
                                              4

presentation? Shouldn't we reward her?" he asked.

　　當我演說結束時，我丈夫的舉動令我和全班同學十分驚訝。他問大家：「你們難道不覺得史區特女士講解得很精彩嗎？我們是不是該獎勵她呢？」

　　presentation〔,prɛzn̩'teʃən〕*n.* 發表；表現　　reward〔rɪ'wɔrd〕*v.* 獎賞

I expected a polite round *of applause*, *but* instead, my *nor-*

mally reserved husband swept me *into his arms and* kissed me.

"That, students, is reinforcement," he told the stunned onlookers.
                                                          5

"Class dismissed."

　　本來我以為大家會很有禮貌地鼓掌，但出乎我意料之外，我那位素來十分內向的丈夫卻一把抱住我，並親吻我。「同學們，這就是一種獎勵，」他對那些目瞪口呆的學生說。「下課。」

　　round〔raʊnd〕*n.* 一陣；一回合　　applause〔ə'plɔz〕*n.* 鼓掌
　　normally〔'nɔrml̩ɪ〕*adv.* 通常　　reserved〔rɪ'zɜvd〕*adj.* 內向的
　　sweep〔swip〕*v.* 用力拉；橫掃　　reinforcement〔,riɪn'forsmənt〕*n.* 加強
　　onlooker〔'ɑn,lʊkə〕*n.* 旁觀者　　dismiss〔dɪs'mɪs〕*v.* 下（課）；解散

4. (**A**) *do a good job* 「做得很好」，由於事情發生在過去，須用過去式動詞，故選 (A) *did*。

5. (**D**) (A) interesting〔'ɪntərɪstɪŋ〕*adj.* 有趣的
　　　　　 (B) frightening〔'fraɪtn̩ɪŋ〕*adj.* 可怕的
　　　　　 (C) contented〔kən'tɛntɪd〕*adj.* 滿足的
　　　　　 (D) *stunned*〔stʌnd〕*adj.* 嚇呆的

TEST 23

Read the following passage, and choose the best answer for each blank.

Lung cancer is one of the most deadly diseases in the U.S. More than 100,000 Americans die each year ___1___ lung cancer. Keeping away from cigarettes, of course, is the best protective measure to take. ___2___ scientists may have found ___3___ way to prevent lung cancer. The secret is for people ___4___ carrots, spinach, or other vegetables every day.

___5___ can vegetables stop cancer? Foods ___6___ carrots, spinach, and tomatoes contain a form of vitamin A ___7___ carotene. The body uses carotene to help form the tissue that lines the lungs. So doctors have thought ___8___ might be a connection between eating foods containing carotene and preventing the disease.

Doctors in Chicago ___9___ this connection for more than 20 years. The doctors' findings have shown an interesting pattern: those men who eat the ___10___ carotene have had fewer cases of lung cancer than those who eat little carotene.

1. A. on
   B. for
   C. at
   D. of

2. A. But
   B. Unless
   C. If
   D. Until

3. A. each
   B. another
   C. other
   D. every

4. A. eat
   B. ate
   C. to eat
   D. eating

5. A. Which
   B. When
   C. What
   D. How

6. A. such as
   B. as if
   C. as like
   D. likewise

7. A. calling
   B. is called
   C. called
   D. calls

8. A. there
   B. here
   C. it
   D. they

9. A. had tested
   B. are testing
   C. would have tested
   D. have been testing

10. A. better
    B. more
    C. worst
    D. most

TEST 23 詳解

Lung cancer is one *of the most deadly diseases* in the U.S.

More than 100,000 Americans die *each year* *of lung cancer.*

Keeping away from cigarettes, *of course*, is the *best* protective
1

measure *to take.* ***But*** scientists may have found another way *to*
2   3

prevent lung cancer. The secret is for people to eat carrots, spin-
4

ach, *or* other vegetables *every day.*

在美國，肺癌是最嚴重的致命疾病之一。每年都有超過十萬個美國人死於肺癌。當然，遠離香煙是所能採取的最佳防護措施。但是科學家可能已經發現了另一種預防肺癌的方法。這個祕訣就是，人們每天都要吃胡蘿蔔、菠菜或其他蔬菜。

> lung (lʌŋ) *n.* 肺　　deadly ('dɛdlɪ) *adj.* 致命的
> protective (prə'tɛktɪv) *adj.* 保護的　　measure ('mɛʒɚ) *n.* 措施
> carrot ('kærət) *n.* 胡蘿蔔　　spinach ('spɪnɪdʒ) *n.* 菠菜

1. (**D**) 指死於某種疾病，用「*die of* + 疾病」表示。

2. (**A**) 依句意，選 (A) ***But*** 「但是」。而 (B) 除非，(C) 如果，(D) 直到，均與句意不合。

3. (**B**) 依句意，選 (B) ***another*** 「另一個」。而 (A)、(C)、(D) 皆不合句意。

4. (**C**) 不定詞片語 to eat … every day 做主詞 the secret 的補語。

How can vegetables stop cancer? Foods *such as carrots, spin-*
　5　　　　　　　　　　　　　　　　　　　　　　　　6

ach, and tomatoes contain a form *of vitamin A called carotene.*
　　　　　　　　　　　　　　　　　　　　　　7

The body uses carotene to help form the tissue *that lines the*

lungs. **So** doctors have thought *there might be a connection be-*
　　　　　　　　　　　　　　　8

tween eating foods containing carotene **and** *preventing the disease.*

　蔬菜如何能預防癌症呢？像胡蘿蔔、菠菜、蕃茄等食物，含有一種維生素A的成分，稱爲胡蘿蔔素。人體能利用胡蘿蔔素，來幫助形成肺臟的內層組織，因此，醫生們認爲，吃含胡蘿蔔素的食物，和預防這種疾病，可能有關連。

vitamin〔'vaɪtəmɪn〕*n.* 維生素
carotene〔'kærəˌtin〕*n.* 胡蘿蔔素
tissue〔'tɪʃu〕*n.* 組織　　line〔laɪn〕*v.* 做襯底

5. (**D**) 依句意，本問句是問蔬菜「如何」預防癌症，故選 (D) **How**。

6. (**A**) (A) 像是　　(B) 好像　　(C) 無此用法　　(D) 同樣地

7. (**C**) a form of vitamin A called carotene 是由 a form of vitamin A which is called carotene 簡化而來。

8. (**A**) 依句意，表示「有」關連，須用「**there** + be 動詞」，選 (A)。

Doctors *in Chicago* have been testing this connection *for more*
9

than 20 years. The doctors' findings have shown an interesting

pattern: those men *who eat the most carotene* have had fewer cases
10

of lung cancer **than** *those* **who** *eat little carotene*.

芝加哥的醫生一直在測試這種關連，已經二十多年了。醫生們的發現，顯示出一種有趣的模式：那些攝取最多胡蘿蔔素的人，比那些僅攝取少量胡蘿蔔素的人，較少罹患肺癌。

finding〔ˋfaɪndɪŋ〕*n.* 發現　　case〔kes〕*n.* 病例

9. (**D**) 表「從過去一直持續到現在，而且仍在進行的動作」，要用「現在完成進行式」，其公式為「have been＋V-ing」，故選 (D)。

10. (**D**) 依句意，攝取「最多量的」胡蘿蔔素，應選 (D) *most*「最多的」。

TEST 24

Read the following passage, and choose the best answer for each blank.

While ___1___ on an old English farm, I discussed the problem with the owners of the large stone step ___2___ into the kitchen. Over the years, the center of the stone had become worn down, and rain formed a puddle ___3___.

Understandably, the owners wanted to retain the historic entrance, so I ___4___ that we dig the stone out, turn it over and use the bottom for the top. After much heaving and straining, we discovered that the farmer's grandfather had done ___5___ that a half-century earlier.

1. A. stayed
   B. staying
   C. was stayed
   D. was staying

2. A. leading
   B. wandering
   C. to lead
   D. to wander

3. A. later
   B. after
   C. since
   D. there

4. A. said
   B. implied
   C. suggested
   D. announced

5. A. so
   B. such
   C. likely
   D. exactly

TEST 24 詳解

While *staying* on an old English farm, I discussed the problem
　　　　　1

with the owners of the large stone step *leading* into the kitchen.
　　　　　　　　　　　　　　　　　　　　　　　2

Over the years, the center of the stone had become worn down,

and rain formed a puddle *there*.
　　　　　　　　　　3

　　當我住在一座古老的英國農場時，和農場主人討論，有關通往廚房那塊巨
型石階的問題。多年來，石階的中間部份都磨損了，而且雨水也在那裏形成了
小水坑。

> **over the years** 多年來
> 　(over the night 整夜，over the next month 下個月一整個月)
> **wear down** 磨損　　puddle〔'pʌdḷ〕*n.* 水坑

1. (**B**) 從屬連接詞 if, when, while, though, as, than, unless 等引導的
　　　　子句中，句意明確時，可省略主詞與 be 動詞，故原句是由 While I was
　　　　staying…，省略主詞 I 與 be 動詞 was 而來，故選 (B) *staying*。

2. (**A**) 空格是由形容詞子句 which led into…省略關代而來的分詞片語，
　　　　選 (A) *leading*。　**lead (in)to** ~　通往~
　　　　而 (B) wander〔'wɑndɚ〕*v.* 徘徊，不合句意。

3. (**D**) 依句意，選 (D) *there*「（在）那裏」。
　　　　而 (A) 後來，(B) 在~之後，(C) 自從，皆不合句意。

Understandably, the owners wanted to retain the historic entrance, *so* I suggested *that* we dig the stone out, turn it over *and*
4

use the bottom for the top. *After much heaving and straining,* we discovered *that* the farmer's grandfather had done exactly that a
5

half-century earlier.

理所當然地，農場主人想要保存這有歷史性的入口，所以我建議將石頭挖出來，把它翻過來，用底部來取代頂端。在用力拉扯，並抬起石頭之後，我們才發現，早在半個世紀前，農場主人的祖父就用過這個方法了。

understandably (͵ʌndɚ'stændəblɪ) *adv.* 理所當然地
entrance ('ɛntrəns) *n.* 入口　　retain (rɪ'ten) *v.* 保存
historic (hɪs'tɔrɪk) *adj.* 有歷史性的
dig (dɪg) *v.* 挖掘　　*use* A *for* B　用 A 取代 B
heave (hiv) *v.* 舉起　　strain (stren) *v.* 用力拉

4. (**C**)　由於空格後動詞 dig 為原形動詞，故選 (C) *suggested*。suggest 為慾望動詞，其句型為：「慾望動詞 (如 suggest, order, require 等) + that + 主詞 + (should) + 原形 V.」。而 (A) say「說」，(B) imply (ɪm'plaɪ) *v.* 暗示，(D) announce (ə'naʊns) *v.* 宣佈，則無此用法。

5. (**D**)　依句意，選 (D) *exactly* (ɪg'zæktlɪ) *adv.* 正是；恰好。

TEST 25

Read the following passage, and choose the best answer for each blank.

Reports of people being killed by sharks are sometimes heard, and such reports ___1___ the fear that many humans have of sharks. The shark that is feared ___2___ is the great white shark, often viewed ___3___ a monster fish. Without a ___4___, the great white shark can be extremely dangerous to people. ___5___, say scientists who study the animal, our fears of it are far out of ___6___ to the actual danger of the animal. Such fears are ___7___ on myths about great white sharks, myths that result from a lack of understanding. ___8___ the great white shark's reputation, it only occasionally attacks people and ___9___ kills them. Since 1926, ___10___ only sixty-eight reported shark attacks on people off the West Coast of the United States.

1. A. were strengthening
   B. are strengthened
   C. had strengthened
   D. strengthen

2. A. the most
   B. the best
   C. the highest
   D. the biggest

3. A. like
   B. for
   C. as
   D. of

4. A. reason
   B. mercy
   C. purpose
   D. doubt

5. A. Then
   B. But
   C. Therefore
   D. So

6. A. production
   B. projection
   C. proportion
   D. protection

7. A. based
   B. counted
   C. focused
   D. touched

8. A. Although
   B. Unless
   C. Despite
   D. Whether

9. A. simply
   B. rarely
   C. really
   D. only

10. A. it has
    B. there were
    C. there seems to be
    D. there have been

TEST 25 詳解

Reports *of people being killed by sharks* are *sometimes* heard,

and such reports strengthen the fear *that many humans have of*
                    1

sharks. The shark *that is feared the most* is the great white shark,
                                        2

often viewed as a monster fish. *Without a doubt*, the great white
            3   4

shark can be *extremely* dangerous to people. *But*, say scientists
                                                  5

who study the animal, our fears *of it* are *far* out of proportion to
                                                            6

the actual danger *of the animal*.

鯊魚咬死人的報導時有所聞，而這樣的報導加深了許多人對鯊魚的恐懼。
人們最害怕的鯊魚是大白鯊，大白鯊通常被認為是像怪獸的魚。無疑地，大白
鯊對人類而言，是非常危險的。但是，研究大白鯊的科學家指出，人們對大白
鯊的恐懼，和大白鯊實際的危險性相比，是非常不成比例的。

shark〔ʃɑrk〕*n.* 鯊魚　　monster〔'mɑnstɚ〕*n.* 怪獸
extremely〔ɪk'strimlɪ〕*adv.* 非常地　　actual〔'æktʃʊəl〕*adj.* 實際的

1. (**D**) 依句意，報導「加深」許多人的恐懼，應為主動，而依句意為現在式，
故選 (D) *strengthen*〔'strɛŋθən〕*v.* 加強。

2. (**A**) 此處用最高級副詞，修飾動詞 fear，表示「最」怕，用 *the most*，
選 (A)。而 (B) 最好，(C) 最高，(D) 最大，均不合。

3. (**C**) *view* A *as* B 把 A 視為 B

4. (**D**) *without a doubt* 無疑地
   (A) reason〔ˈrizn̩〕 *n.* 理由
   (B) mercy〔ˈmɝsɪ〕 *n.* 慈悲 without mercy 毫不留情地
   (C) purpose〔ˈpɝpəs〕 *n.* 目的

5. (**B**) 依句意，前後語氣有轉折，故選 (B) *But*。

6. (**C**) *out of proportion to* ～ 與～不成比例
   proportion〔prəˈporʃən, -ˈpɔr-〕 *n.* 比例
   (A) production〔prəˈdʌkʃən〕 *n.* 生產
   (B) projection〔prəˈdʒɛkʃən〕 *n.* 投射
   (D) protection〔prəˈtɛkʃən〕 *n.* 保護

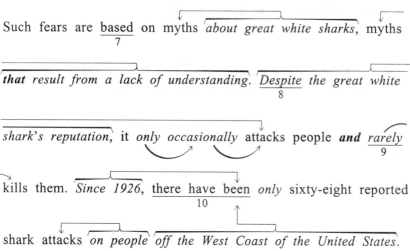

Such fears are <u>based</u> on myths *about great white sharks*, myths
        7

that result from a lack of understanding. <u>Despite</u> *the great white*
             8

shark's reputation, it *only occasionally* attacks people *and* <u>*rarely*</u>
                    9

kills them. *Since 1926*, <u>there have been</u> *only* sixty-eight reported
           10

shark attacks *on people off the West Coast of the United States.*
這樣的恐懼是來自與大白鯊有關的傳聞，而傳聞則源於缺乏了解。儘管大白鯊
惡名昭彰，但牠只是偶爾攻擊人類，而且很少咬死他們。自一九二六年以來，
在美國西岸外海，只有六十八件鯊魚攻擊人類的報導。

> myth〔mɪθ〕*n.* 神話；傳聞　　***result from*** 由於
> lack〔læk〕*n.* 缺乏　　　reputation〔͵rɛpjə'teʃən〕*n.* 名聲
> occasionally〔ə'keʒənḷɪ〕*adv.* 偶爾
> attack〔ə'tæk〕*v. , n.* 攻擊

7. (**A**) ***be based on*** 根據
   (B) count〔kaʊnt〕*v.* 數；計算　　(C) focus〔'fokəs〕*v.* 集中
   (D) touch〔tʌtʃ〕*v.* 碰觸

8. (**C**) 依句意，「僅管」大白鯊惡名昭彰，且空格後為名詞，故選介系詞
   (C) ***Despite***。而 (A) Although 為連接詞，須接子句，用法不合。
   (B) 除非，(D) 是否，則不合句意。

9. (**B**) (A) simply〔'sɪmplɪ〕*adv.* 只是；簡單地
   (B) ***rarely***〔'rɛrlɪ〕*adv.* 很少
   (C) really〔'rɪəlɪ〕*adv.* 真正地；確實
   (D) 只有

10. (**D**) 有連接詞 since 時，主要子句須用現在完成式，且「there + be 動
    詞」表「有；存在」，故選 (D) ***there have been***。

TEST 26

Read the following passage, and choose the best answer for each blank.

Controlling air pollution is another ___1___ objective.
Without food, man can live for about five weeks; without water
about five days. Without air, he can only live five minutes, so
pure air is a ___2___. Here the wrongdoer is the automobile.
___3___ there is a concentration of automobiles, as in our big
cities, air pollution is severe. It is important to see ___4___ our
cars are equipped with pollution-control devices. Such devices
effectively reduce the harmful gases ___5___ from the engine.

1. A. temporary
   B. crucial
   C. short-term
   D. economic

2. A. slogan
   B. must
   C. right
   D. blessing

3. A. Though
   B. Since
   C. Where
   D. As

4. A. that
   B. whether
   C. how
   D. it

5. A. emit
   B. emits
   C. emitted
   D. emitting

TEST 26 詳解

Controlling air pollution is another <u>crucial</u> objective. *Without*
1

food, man can live *for about five weeks*; *without water* about five

days. *Without air*, he can only live *five minutes*, *so* pure air is a

<u>must</u>. Here the wrongdoer is the automobile.
2

控制空氣污染是另外一個重要的目標。人沒有食物,可以活大約五週;沒
有水,可以活大約五天。沒有空氣,則只能活五分鐘。所以純淨的空氣是絕對
需要的。而眼前的肇禍者就是汽車。

objective〔əb'dʒɛktɪv〕*n.* 目標　　pure〔pjʊr〕*adj.* 純淨的
wrongdoer〔'rɔŋ'duɚ〕*n.* 爲害者;做壞事的人
automobile〔ˌɔtə'mobɪl〕*n.* 汽車

1. (**B**) *crucial*〔'kruʃəl〕*adj.* 非常重要的
　　(A) temporary〔'tɛmpəˌrɛrɪ〕*adj.* 暫時的
　　(C) short-term〔'ʃɔrt'tɝm〕*adj.* 短期的
　　(D) economic〔ˌikə'namɪk〕*adj.* 經濟的

2. (**B**) *must*〔mʌst〕*n.* 絕對需要的東西
　　(A) slogan〔'slogən〕*n.* 口號
　　(C) right〔raɪt〕*n.* 權利
　　(D) blessing〔'blɛsɪŋ〕*n.* 幸福

__Where__ there is a concentration of automobiles, __as__ in our big cities,
   3

air pollution is severe. It is important to see __that__ our cars are
                        4

equipped with pollution-control devices. Such devices effectively re-

duce the harmful gases emitted from the engine.
                   5

就像我們這裡的大都市一樣，只要汽車集中的地方，空氣污染就很嚴重。重要的是，我們要注意，汽車上必須要有控制空氣污染的裝置。這種裝置，可以有效地減少引擎所排放的有害氣體。

> concentration〔͵kɑnsn̩'treʃən〕 *n.* 集中　　severe〔sə'vɪr〕 *adj.* 嚴重的
> *__be equipped with__* 裝備有～　　device〔dɪ'vaɪs〕 *n.* 裝置
> effectively〔ə'fɛktɪvlɪ〕 *adv.* 有效地

3. (**C**) where 在此作表地點的從屬連接詞，表「在～的地方」，引導副詞子句，修飾動詞 is。而 (A) Though「雖然」，不合句意；(B) Since 和 (D) As，均可表「由於」，和後面的 as in our big cities 句意不合，故不選。

4. (**A**) *see that ～* 注意～；務必～
　　　 see 之後加 that 子句時，雖然有「應該」的意思，但 that 子句中不必出現 should 來表「應該」。

5. (**C**) 原句為… gases *which are* emitted from the engine.因關代和 be 動詞可同時省略，故選 (C) *__emitted__*。
　　　 emit〔ɪ'mɪt〕 *v.* 排放

TEST 27

Read the following passage, and choose the best answer for each blank.

Books are to mankind ___1___ memory is to the individual.
They contain the history of our race, the discoveries we have
made, the ___2___ knowledge and experience of ages; they ___3___
for us the marvels and beauties of nature; help us in our difficulties;
comfort us in sorrow and suffering; change hours of weariness
___4___ moments of delight; ___5___ our minds with ideas, fill them
with good and happy thoughts, and lift us ___6___ ourselves.

When we read, we may ___7___ be kings and live in palaces,
but, what is better, we may ___8___ ourselves to the mountains or
the seashore, and visit the most beautiful parts of the earth, without
fatigue, inconvenience or expense. Precious and priceless ___9___
the blessings which books scatter around our daily paths. We walk
___10___ imagination, with the noblest spirits, through the most
sublime and enchanting regions.

1. A. that
   B. which
   C. what
   D. those

2. A. accumulated
   B. accumulating
   C. calculated
   D. calculating

3. A. make
   B. give
   C. picture
   D. take

4. A. in
   B. up to
   C. for
   D. into

5. A. store
   B. keep
   C. leave
   D. get

6. A. upon
   B. out of and above
   C. out
   D. into and out

7. A. not
   B. possibly
   C. not only
   D. as well as

8. A. imagine
   B. transport
   C. deliver
   D. make

9. A. is
   B. do
   C. have
   D. are

10. A. in
    B. for
    C. on
    D. with

TEST 27 詳解

Books are to mankind ***what*** memory is to the individual. They
1

contain the history *of our race*, the discoveries *we have made*, the

accumulated knowledge and experience *of ages*; they picture *for us*
2   3

the marvels and beauties *of nature*; help us *in our difficulties*;

comfort us *in sorrow and suffering*; change hours *of weariness* into
4

moments *of delight*; store our minds *with ideas*, fill them *with*
5

good and happy thoughts, ***and*** lift us *out of and above* ourselves.
6

書之於人類，猶如回憶之於個人。書中包含了我們人類的歷史、我們的發
現，以及歷代所累積的知識及經驗；書為我們描繪了自然的奇蹟和美麗；在困
難中幫助我們；在憂傷和苦難中安慰我們；將困倦的時光化作欣喜的時刻；以
各種概念來充實我們的心靈，使之充滿良善和快樂的思想，並且提升我們以超
越自己。

mankind〔mæn'kaɪnd〕*n.* 人類　　individual〔,ɪndə'vɪdʒuəl〕*n.* 個人
contain〔kən'ten〕*v.* 包含　　age〔edʒ〕*n.* 時代
marvel〔'marvḷ〕*n.* 奇蹟　　comfort〔'kʌmfət〕*v.* 安慰
sorrow〔'saro〕*n.* 悲傷　　suffering〔'sʌfərɪŋ〕*n.* 苦難
weariness〔'wɪrɪnɪs〕*n.* 疲勞　　lift〔lɪft〕*v.* 提升

2. (**A**) 知識和經驗應是「被」累積而成的，故選 (A) ***accumulated*** ，過去
分詞當形容詞用。　　 accumulate〔ə'kjumjə,let〕*v.* 累積
(C) (D) 為 calculate〔'kælkjə,let〕*v.* 計算 的過去分詞與現在分詞，均
與句意不合。

3. (**C**) picture 在此做動詞用，指「描寫」。

4. (**D**) ***change*** A (***in***)***to*** B 把 A 變成 B

5. (**A**) 依句意，應選 (A) ***store***〔stor , stɔr〕*v.* 儲存；裝滿。

6. (**B**) 依句意，選 (B) ***out of and above*** ourselves「提升並超越我們自己」。

When *we read*, we may ***not only*** be kings and live *in palaces*,
　　　　　　　　　　　　　　　7

***but*, *what* *is* *better*,** we may transport ourselves *to the mountains or*
　　　　　　　　　　　　　　8

the seashore, ***and*** visit the *most* beautiful parts *of the earth, without*

fatigue, inconvenience or expense.

　　當我們閱讀的時候，我們不只可以當國王，住在宮殿裏，尤有甚者，我們
可以把自己送到山上或海邊，造訪地球上最美的地方，而無須勞苦不便，或是
花費金錢。

　　　palace〔'pælɪs〕*n.* 宮殿　　seashore〔'si,ʃor〕*n.* 海邊
　　　fatigue〔fə'tig〕*n.* 疲勞　　inconvenience〔,ɪnkən'vinjəns〕*n.* 不方便
　　　expense〔ɪk'spɛns〕*n.* 費用

7. (**C**) ***not only*** ⋯ ***but*** (***also***) ～　不僅⋯而且～

8. (**B**) ***transport*** 〔 træns'port , -'port 〕*v.* 運送

　　而 (A) imagine 〔 ɪ'mædʒɪn 〕*v.* 想像，加受詞之後，可接不定詞 to-
　　V. ，但不可接介詞 to ；(C) deliver 〔 dɪ'lɪvə 〕*v.* 遞送 (物品) ，
　　(D) make 「製造」，用法與句意皆不合。

Precious and priceless <u>are</u> the blessings *which books scatter*
9

around our daily paths. We walk <u>*in imagination,*</u> *with the noblest*
10

spirits, *through the most sublime and enchanting regions.*

書本在我們日常生活中所散播的好處，是寶貴而無價的。我們以最高貴的精神，
在想像中行進，穿過最莊嚴、最迷人的境界。

> precious 〔'prɛʃəs 〕*adj.* 珍貴的
> priceless 〔'praɪslɪs 〕*adj.* 無價的
> blessing 〔'blɛsɪŋ 〕*n.* 值得感謝的事
> scatter 〔'skætə 〕*v.* 散播　　path 〔 pæθ 〕*n.* 道路；途徑
> sublime 〔 sə'blaɪm 〕*adj.* 莊嚴的
> enchanting 〔 ɪn'tʃæntɪŋ 〕*adj.* 迷人的
> region 〔'ridʒən 〕*n.* 地區；境界

9. (**D**) 本句為一倒裝句，主詞 the blessings 為複數，又主詞補語 precious
　　and priceless 為形容詞，故選 (D) ***are*** 。

10. (**A**) ***in*** imagination　在想像中

TEST 28

Read the following passage, and choose the best answer for each blank.

In the past, people ___1___ had as much leisure time as we ___2___ now. Traditionally, work ___3___ so much time that very little ___4___ for any sort of recreation. Fortunately, life has changed. With more free time today, most of us are able to pursue other interests. We have a great many choices: music, dance, drama, movies, sports, travels and so on. Of course, the choices ___5___ on personal tastes and preferences.

1. A. usually
   B. mostly
   C. rarely
   D. always

2. A. are
   B. have
   C. had
   D. did

3. A. spent
   B. cost
   C. needed
   D. took

4. A. left
   B. was left
   C. was remained
   D. was reminded

5. A. depend
   B. are depended
   C. are dependence
   D. are independent

TEST 28 詳解

In the past, people $\underset{1}{\underline{rarely}}$ had *as* much leisure time $\overline{as}$ *we*

$\overline{have\ now}$. *Traditionally*, work $\underset{3}{\underline{took}}$ *so* much time $\overline{that}$ *very little*

$\underset{4}{\underline{was\ left}}$ *for any sort of recreation.*

從前，人們很少有像我們今天所擁有的，這麼多的休閒時間。依照傳統，
工作花去大部分時間，極少有剩餘的時間，來從事娛樂活動。

leisure ('liʒɚ) *adj.* 空閒的　　sort (sɔrt) *n.* 種類
recreation (,rɛkrɪ'eʃən) *n.* 娛樂

1. (**C**) (A) 通常　　　　　　　　(B) mostly ('mostlɪ) *adv.* 大多
　　　　(C) *rarely* ('rɛrlɪ) *adv.* 很少　(D) 總是

2. (**B**) 同類才能相比，故須用相同之動詞 have 或 had，由 now 可知，應選
　　　　(B) *have*。

3. (**D**) 「事情＋take＋時間」表「某事花費多少時間」，故選 (D) *took*。
　　　　而 (A) spend，須以人為主詞，(B) cost 指「花費多少錢」，(C) 無此
　　　　用法。

4. (**B**) that 引導之名詞子句的主詞為 time，為避免重複，予以省略，且依句
　　　　意，為被動語態，故選 (B) *was left*。
　　　　(C) remain (rɪ'men) *v.* 仍然是，(D) remind (rɪ'maɪnd) *v.* 使想起，
　　　　用法、句意均不合。

Fortunately, life has changed. *With more free time today*, most

of us are able to pursue other interests. We have a great many

choices: music, dance, drama, movies, sports, travels and so on.

Of course, the choices <u>depend</u> on personal tastes and preferences.
　　　　　　　　　　　　5

很幸運地，生活型態改變了。由於現在空閒時間較多，我們大部分的人，都能
做其他自己有興趣的事。我們有很多選擇：如音樂、跳舞、戲劇、電影、運動、
旅遊等等。當然，這些選擇是依個人的興趣及偏好而定。

　　　pursue〔pɚ'su〕*v.* 追求；從事　　***and so on*** 等等
　　　taste〔test〕*n.* 興趣；愛好　　preference〔'prɛfərəns〕*n.* 偏好

5.(**A**) 依句意，選 (A) ***depend on***「視～而定」。
　　　dependence〔dɪ'pɛndəns〕*n.* 依賴
　　　independent〔͵ɪndɪ'pɛndənt〕*adj.* 獨立的

TEST 29

Read the following passage, and choose the best answer for each blank.

Walking may not seem fascinating, but it can be. When you walk, you move slowly, ___1___ you can see the world ___2___ you. Walking is great because you can do ___3___ anytime and anywhere. An evening walk ___4___ the streets of a big city can be ___5___ as enjoyable as a morning stroll ___6___ a country road or a hike in the mountains. ___7___ addition, you don't need any fancy equipment ___8___ participate in this activity. If you have a good pair of shoes, you're ready to go. Another benefit of this pastime is ___9___ you can enjoy it with friends or alone. You ___10___ don't have to worry about winning or losing. Just getting there is enough.

1. A. so
   B. if
   C. that
   D. as

2. A. around
   B. between
   C. above
   D. besides

3. A. on
   B. in
   C. to
   D. it

4. A. from
   B. over
   C. across
   D. through

5. A. even
   B. ever
   C. just
   D. like

6. A. of
   B. on
   C. at
   D. to

7. A. For
   B. In
   C. By
   D. On

8. A. in
   B. up
   C. with
   D. to

9. A. which
   B. where
   C. that
   D. what

10. A. also
    B. either
    C. neither
    D. too

TEST 29 詳解

Walking may not seem fascinating, ***but*** it can be. ***When you walk***, you move *slowly*, ***so*** you can see the world *around you*.

1   2

Walking is great ***because*** you can do it *anytime* ***and*** *anywhere*.

3

An evening walk *through the streets* *of a big city* can be just *as*

4   5

enjoyable *as a morning stroll on a country road* ***or*** *a hike in the*

6

mountains.

　　散步也許不是那麼吸引人，但它可以變得如此。散步時，你會慢慢地走動，所以可以看看周遭的世界。散步是一件很棒的事，因為隨時隨地都可以散步。在傍晚時，沿著大城市的街道散步，就如同清晨在鄉間小路上漫步，或是像到山上健行，一樣地樂趣無窮。

　　　　fascinating (ˈfæsn̩ˌetɪŋ) *adj.* 吸引人的
　　　　enjoyable (ɪnˈdʒɔɪəbl̩) *adj.* 快樂的
　　　　stroll (strol) *n.* 漫步　　hike (haɪk) *n.* 健行

1. (**A**) 依句意，空格應填一表結果的連接詞，故選 (A) ***so*** 「所以」。
　　而 (B) if 「如果」，(C) 關代 that 之前不可有逗點，而且也沒有先行詞，
　　(D) as 「由於」，均不合。

2. (**A**) 依句意，選 (A) ***around*** 「在～周圍」。而 (B) between 「二者之間」，
　　(C) above 「在～之上」，(D) besides 「除了～之外」，均不合句意。

3. (**D**) 時間副詞 anytime 之前不可接介系詞，故 (A)(B)(C) 不選。
　　　(D) it 指 walking，當 do 的受詞。

4. (**D**) 依句意，選 (D) ***walk through*** 「沿著～散步」。而 (A) 沒有 walk
　　　from 的用法，(B) walk over 「（由於沒有對手而）獨自跑步；輕易
　　　取勝」，(C) walk across 「橫越」，均不合句意。

5. (**C**) (A) 甚至　　　　　　　　　(B) 曾經
　　　(C) 就；正好　　　　　　　(D) 像是（因句中已有 as，故不可選）

6. (**B**) ***stroll on a road*** 在路上漫步

In addition, you don't need any fancy equipment *to participate in*
――7――　　　　　　　　　　　　　　　　　　　　　　　　――8――

this activity. **If you have a good pair of shoes,** you're ready to go.

Another benefit *of this pastime* is ***that*** you can enjoy *it with*
　　　　　　　　　　　　　　　　　　　　　――9――

friends or alone. You *also* don't have to worry about winning or
　　　　　　　　　　　――10――

losing. *Just* getting there is enough.

此外，參與這項活動，你不需要任何昂貴的裝備。如果有一雙好鞋，你就可以
上路了。這項消遣的另一種好處，就是你可以與朋友分享散步的樂趣，或者獨
自享受。你也無須擔心輸贏。只要到達那裏就夠了。

　　　fancy（'fænsɪ）*adj.* 昂貴的；花俏的
　　　equipment（ɪ'kwɪpmənt）*n.* 設備；裝備
　　　participate（pə'tɪsə,pet）*v.* 參與（與 in 連用）
　　　benefit（'bɛnəfɪt）*n.* 好處　　　pastime（'pæs,taɪm）*n.* 消遣

7. (**B**) *in addition* 此外

8. (**D**) need + 受詞 + to-V 「需要~以…」

9. (**C**) 動詞 is 後爲一名詞子句，應由 that 來引導，故選 (C)。而 (A) 關代 which 只能引導形容詞子句，不能引導名詞子句，(B) where 爲表 地點的關係副詞，(D) what (= *the thing that*) 爲一複合關代， 在此用法不合。

10. (**A**) 依句意，選 (A) *also* 「也」。而 (B) either 表「也」時，不可放句中； (C) neither 「也不」，本身即有否定含意，不須與 not 連用，而 (D) too 表「也」時，只用於肯定句，在此不合。

TEST 30

Read the following passage, and choose the best answer for each blank.

Competition presupposes that some must win and ___1___ must lose. Competition is ___2___, with only a small percentage of the participants ___3___ to the top. Those who ___4___ their goals feel they are successful; often those who do not may view themselves ___5___ failures.

1. A. other
   B. another
   C. others
   D. the other

2. A. weak
   B. keen
   C. violent
   D. satisfactory

3. A. rising
   B. rise
   C. raising
   D. raise

4. A. fail
   B. aim
   C. reach
   D. attend

5. A. for
   B. upon
   C. with
   D. as

TEST 30 詳解

Competition presupposes *that some must win **and** others must*
$\overline{\qquad\qquad}$
1

lose. Competition is <u>keen</u>, *with only a small percentage of the par-*
2

ticipants rising to the top.
3

凡競賽必然有輸贏。競賽是激烈的，因爲只有參賽者中的極小部分，能得
到最高的榮譽。

> competition〔͵kɑmpə'tɪʃən〕*n.* 競爭；比賽
> presuppose〔͵prisə'poz〕*v.* 假定；以～爲前提
> percentage〔pə'sɛntɪdʒ〕*n.* 百分比
> participant〔pə'tɪsəpənt〕*n.* 參與者

1. (**C**) *some* … *others* ~ 有些…有些～
   而 (A) other 是形容詞，之後須接複數名詞，(B) another 是指三者以
   上的另一個，(D) the other 是指二者中的另一個，用法皆不合。

2. (**B**) violent 和 keen 均可表「激烈的」，但指「競爭激烈」，只能用 keen。
   (A) 虛弱的，(D) 令人滿意的，則不合句意。

Those ***who*** <u>reach</u> *their goals* feel *they are successful*; *often* those
4

who *do not* may view themselves <u>as</u> failures.
5

達到目標的人，會覺得自己是成功的；而那些未達到目標的人，常會認爲自己是
失敗者。

> goal〔gol〕*n.* 目標   failure〔'feljə〕*n.* 失敗的人

3. (**A**)　「with＋受詞＋現在分詞」可用來表附帶狀況，依句意，選 (A) *rising*。

　　　　rise〔raɪz〕*v.* 上升；地位升高　　*rise to the top* 成為佼佼者

　　　　而 (C)，(D) raise〔rez〕*v.* 提高，則不合句意。

4. (**C**)　*reach one's goal* 達到目標　　aim〔em〕*v.* 瞄準

5. (**D**)　*view ~ as …* 把~看成是…

┌──────《克漏字答題技巧》──────────────────┐

　　　克漏字考試，不是考句意，就是考文法。如 (A)(B)(C)(D) 四組，
文字大致相同，但排列不同，就是考文法。如 (A)(B)(C)(D) 文字均
不同，即是考句意，注意上下文句意，選一個合句意，而且比較合
乎常理的答案。如果題目不會做，就唸一唸，看哪一個比較順，就
選哪一個。題目做多了，你自然就有選正確答案的語感。

└──┘

TEST 31

Read the following passage, and choose the best answer for each blank.

I am sitting on the riverbank, feeling very unhappy. My wet clothes are ___1___ a heap next to me. I'm ___2___ in Dad's warm, dry blanket. But I feel ___3___. I wish I ___4___ fishing today.

Two hours ago, I was standing ___5___ a small rock by the river, ___6___. I was waiting for a fish to bite. Dad was nearby. Then it ___7___. I felt a tug on the line. I thought I had a fish. I got ___8___ and lost my footing.

I fell into the river. I'm a good swimmer. Still Dad had to jump in to help me ___9___. I was wet and angry. Dad said to me, "Kevin, today is ___10___."

I'm still angry now. I lost my best fishing rod in that river. And I still don't know if I really had a fish on my line.

1. A. in
   B. at
   C. on
   D. to

2. A. wrap
   B. wrapping
   C. wrapped
   D. to wrap

3. A. damply
   B. damp
   C. damping
   D. dampness

4. A. didn't go
   B. haven't gone
   C. don't go
   D. hadn't gone

5. A. in top of
   B. on top of
   C. from top of
   D. to top of

6. A. fishing
   B. fish
   C. fished
   D. to fish

7. A. vanished
   B. advanced
   C. happened
   D. appeared

8. A. excited
   B. excite
   C. exciting
   D. to excite

9. A. over
   B. out
   C. with
   D. for

10. A. not your time
    B. not your day
    C. not your luck
    D. not your turn

TEST 31 詳解

I am sitting *on the riverbank, feeling very unhappy*. My wet

clothes are <u>in</u> a heap next to me. I'm <u>wrapped</u> *in Dad's warm,*
$\overset{}{1}$ $\overset{}{2}$

dry blanket. **But** I feel <u>damp</u>. I wish *I <u>hadn't gone</u> fishing today.*
$\overset{}{3}$ $\overset{}{4}$

我坐在河邊，覺得很鬱悶。我的濕衣服就堆在一旁，身上裹著父親溫暖的
乾毛毯，但還是覺得濕濕的。我真希望今天沒有來釣魚。

* I am sitting on the riverbank, feeling very unhappy.
= I am sitting on the riverbank, and I feel unhappy.

riverbank (ˈrɪvɚˌbæŋk) *n.* 河岸；河堤　　blanket (ˈblæŋkɪt) *n.* 毛毯

1. (**A**) *in a heap* 一堆

2. (**C**) 依句意為被動語態，故選 (C) *wrapped*。　 wrap (ræp) *v.* 包；裹

3. (**B**) feel 之後接形容詞，表示「覺得～」，依句意，選 (B) *damp* (dæmp) *adj.*
　　　　 溼的。

4. (**D**) wish 表未能實現的願望，所以須和假設語氣連用，故選 (D) *hadn't*
　　　　 gone，表與過去事實相反的假設。

Two hours ago, I was standing *on top of a small rock by the*
$\overset{}{5}$

river, fishing. I was waiting for a fish to bite. Dad was nearby.
$\overset{}{6}$

Then it <u>happened</u>. I felt a tug ⌐*on the line.* I thought I *had a fish.*
　　　　　7

I got <u>excited</u> *and* lost my footing.
　　　　8

　　兩個小時前我就站在河邊的小岩石上釣魚，等著魚兒上鉤。父親就在我附近，然後那件事就發生了。我感覺到有東西在拖拉著釣線，我以為釣到了魚，一興奮就失足滑倒了。

　　　　nearby〔'nɪr‚baɪ〕*adj.* 附近的　　tug〔tʌg〕*n.* 拉；拖
　　　　footing〔'fʊtɪŋ〕*n.* 立足點　　　*lose one's footing* 失去立足點

5. (**B**) *on top of* ~　在~的上面

6. (**A**) 此句原為 I was standing on top of …, and I was fishing.
　　　　改為分詞構句時將 and I was 省略，故選 (A)。

7. (**C**) 依句意，那件事就「發生」了，選 (C) *happen*。
　　　　而 (A) 消失，(B) advance〔əd'væns〕*v.* 前進，(D) 出現，則不合句意。

8. (**A**) get 之後接形容詞，可表示「變得~」，選項中的 excited「感到興奮的」，和 exciting「令人興奮的」，是分詞作形容詞用，依句意，選 (A) *excited*。

　　I fell into the river. I'm a good swimmer. *Still* Dad had to

jump in ⌐*to help me* <u>out</u>. I was wet and angry. Dad said to me,
　　　　　　　　　9

"Kevin, today is <u>not your day</u>."
　　　　　　　　10

　　我掉進河裏，雖然善於游泳，但父親還是跳入水中來幫助我上岸。我全身濕透，而且非常生氣。父親說：「凱文，你今天眞倒楣。」

9. (**B**) *help sb. out* 協助某人

10. (**B**) *be one's day* 是某人非常走運的日子
　　　　　　Today is not your day. 表「今天你的運氣不好。」

I'm *still* angry *now*. I lost my best fishing rod *in that river.*

And I *still* don't know *if I really had a fish on my line.*

　　我現在還是覺得很生氣，因為我把我最好的釣竿掉在那條河裏，而且也搞不清楚當時是不是眞的釣到了魚。

　　rod〔rɑd〕*n.* 棒；竿　　*fishing rod* 釣竿

TEST 32

Read the following passage, and choose the best answer for each blank.

　　Being overweight is just as ugly in men as it is in women.
Modern living has ___1___ us to rely on cars and to use ___2___
devices in the home and office more than ever before. Thus,
people lack exercise.

　　The energy value of the food we eat is counted in calories. The
average man ___3___ around 2,500 to 3,000 a day. This ___4___ age,
build and activity. Being overweight occurs when the input of
calories is greater than the output. To lose weight, you must take in
less than you need — when you do this, your ___5___ body fat will
be used for energy.

<table>
<tr><td>

1. A. encouraged
   B. forbidden
   C. discouraged
   D. convinced

</td><td>

4. A. exchanges by
   B. turns in
   C. differs from
   D. varies with

</td></tr>
<tr><td>

2. A. labor-saving
   B. labor-save
   C. labor-saved
   D. labor-saves

</td><td>

5. A. over
   B. more
   C. full
   D. excess

</td></tr>
<tr><td>

3. A. inquires
   B. requires
   C. retains
   D. sustains

</td><td></td></tr>
</table>

TEST 32 詳解

Being overweight is *just as* ugly *in men as it is in women.*

Modern living has <u>encouraged</u> us to rely on cars *and* to use
1

<u>labor-saving</u> devices *in the home and office more than ever before.*
2

Thus, people lack exercise.

男人太胖就像女人太胖一樣地難看。比起從前，現代生活鼓勵使我們很依
賴汽車，並常常運用家中或辦公室內省力的裝置，於是人們便缺乏運動。

> overweight (ˈovɚˈwet) *adj.* 過重的　　ugly (ˈʌglɪ) *adj.* 醜的
> ***rely on*** 依賴 (= *depend on*)　　device (dɪˈvaɪs) *n.* 裝置；器具
> lack (læk) *v.* 缺乏

1. (**A**) (A) ***encourage*** (ɪnˈkɝɪdʒ) *v.* 鼓勵
   　　　encourage sb. to V. 鼓勵某人～
   　　(B) forbid (fɚˈbɪd) *v.* 禁止
   　　　forbid sb. to V. 禁止某人～
   　　(C) discourage sb. from + V-ing 勸某人不要～
   　　(D) convince sb. of + N. 使某人相信～

2. (**A**) ***labor-saving*** (ˈlebɚˌsevɪŋ) *adj.* 省力的
   　　a labor-saving device 省力的裝置
   　　= a device that saves labor

The energy value *of the food we eat* is counted *in calories.*

The average man <u>requires</u> around 2,500 to 3,000 *a day.* This
　　　　　　　　³

<u>varies</u> *with age, build and activity.* Being overweight occurs *when*
　４

*the input of calories is greater **than** the output.* *To lose weight,*

you must take in less ***than** you need* — ***when** you do this,* your

<u>excess</u> body fat will be used *for energy.*
　⁵

　　我們所吃的食物，其所含能量的多寡，是以卡路里來計算。一般人一天大
約需要兩千五到三千卡路里。這會隨年齡、體格，以及所從事的活動而有所不
同。當攝取的熱量比消耗來得多時，就會產生過重的現象。要減肥，就必須吃
得比所需要的少——如此做，你身上過多的脂肪，就會轉而做爲產生能量之用。

calorie〔'kælərı〕*n.* 卡路里（熱量單位）
average〔'ævərɪdʒ〕*adj.* 普通的　　build〔bɪld〕*n.* 體格；體型
input〔'ɪnˏpʊt〕*n.* 投入；輸入　　output〔'aʊtˏpʊt〕*n.* 輸出
lose weight 減肥　　***take in*** 攝取；接受　　fat〔fæt〕*n.* 脂肪

3. (**B**) 依句意，選 (B) ***require*** 〔rɪ'kwaɪr〕*v.* 需要。
　　　　而 (A) inquire〔ɪn'kwaɪr〕*v.* 詢問，(C) retain〔rɪ'ten〕*v.* 保留，
　　　　(D) sustain〔sə'sten〕*v.* 支撐；維持，均不合句意。

4. (**D**) 依句意，選 (D) ***vary with*** ~「隨著~而有所不同」。vary〔'vɛrɪ〕*v.*
　　　　變化。而 (A) exchange〔ɪks'tʃendʒ〕*v.* 交換，(B) turn in 「繳交」，
　　　　(C) differ from 「和~不同」，均不合句意。

5. (**D**) 依句意，選 (D) ***excess*** 〔ɪk'sɛs〕*adj.* 過多的。
　　　　而 (A) 超過，(B) 更多的，(C) 充滿的，均不合句意。

TEST 33

Read the following passage, and choose the best answer for each blank.

Do you become unhappy ___1___ clouds appear? Are you more cheerful on a sunny day ___2___ on a rainy day? Does the weather really cause changes in your moods?

Most of us feel that stormy weather ___3___ us sad, and many psychologists would ___4___: rain or snow can bring on sadness ___5___ depression in some people. Rather than ___6___ blue on a cold day, for example, some people find it difficult to carry ___7___ their daily routine; even going to work or to school becomes a big job. In contrast, a ___8___ day, particularly during the winter, can make people feel happy. When the weather is pleasant, people are friendlier and more willing to help ___9___. But when the weather is too hot and humid, people are ___10___ to become more quarrelsome.

1. A. when
   B. which
   C. where
   D. that

2. A. as
   B. if
   C. than
   D. being

3. A. causes
   B. influences
   C. leads
   D. makes

4. A. admit
   B. assume
   C. agree
   D. argue

5. A. against
   B. and
   C. for
   D. with

6. A. feel
   B. feeling
   C. having felt
   D. to feel

7. A. in
   B. back
   C. away
   D. on

8. A. chilly
   B. cloudy
   C. rainy
   D. sunny

9. A. another
   B. each other
   C. the other
   D. some other

10. A. like
    B. likely
    C. similarly
    D. tend

TEST 33 詳解

Do you become unhappy ***when*** *clouds appear*? Are you *more*
1

cheerful *on a sunny day* ***than*** *on a rainy day*? Does the weather
2

really cause changes *in your moods*?

　　當雲出現的時候,你是不是會變得不高興呢?和雨天比起來,在晴朗的日
子裏,你是不是會比較快樂呢?天氣眞的會改變你的心情嗎?

cheerful〔'tʃɪrfəl〕*adj.* 愉快的　　mood〔mud〕*n.* 心情

1. (**A**) 依句意,選 (A) ***when*** 「當~時候」。

2. (**C**) ***more ~ than*** … 比…更~

Most *of us* feel ***that*** *stormy weather* *makes* *us sad*, ***and*** many
3

psychologists would agree: rain or snow can bring on sadness and
45

depression *in some people*. *Rather than* *feel* *blue on a cold day*, *for*
6

example, some people find it difficult to carry on their daily
7

routine; *even* going to work or to school becomes a big job.

　　我們大多數的人會覺得，暴風雨的天氣會使我們心情不好，而且許多心理學家都同意：下雨或下雪，會使某些人覺得傷心和沮喪。例如，有些人在寒冷的天氣不會覺得憂鬱，但是會覺得，要進行日常事務十分困難；即使是上班或上學，也變成是件十分艱鉅的工作。

> stormy〔'stɔrmɪ〕*adj.* 暴風雨的
> psychologist〔saɪ'kɑlədʒɪst〕*n.* 心理學家
> ***bring on*** 引起；造成　　depression〔dɪ'prɛʃən〕*n.* 沮喪
> blue〔blu〕*adj.* 憂鬱的　　routine〔ru'tin〕*n.* 例行公事
> job〔dʒɑb〕*n.* 費力的工作

3. (**D**) 使役動詞 make + *sb.* + 形容詞，表「使某人～」。
　　(A) cause + *sb.* +to-V.「使某人～」，在此用法不合。(B) influence + *sb.* + to do ～「影響某人做～」，(C) lead *sb.* to-V.「誘使某人～」，句意及用法皆不合。

4. (**C**) 依句意，選 (C) ***agree***〔ə'gri〕*v.* 同意。
　　(A) admit〔əd'mɪt〕*v.* 承認，與 (B) assume〔ə'sjum〕*v.* 假定，其後須接受詞，用法不合。而 (D) argue〔'ɑrgju〕*v.* 爭論，則不合句意。

5. (**B**) 依句意，選 (B) ***and*** 「以及」。

6. (**A**) ***Rather than*** + 原形 V. (= *Instead of* + *V-ing*) 表「不…(而～)」，故選 (A) ***feel*** 。

7. (**D**) ***carry on*** 進行

In contrast, a <u>sunny</u> day, *particularly during the winter*, can make
　　　　　　8

people feel happy. ***When** the weather is pleasant*, people are friend-

lier ***and more*** willing to help <u>each other</u>. ***But** when the weather is
　　　　　　　　　　　　　　9

too hot and humid, people are <u>likely</u> to become *more* quarrelsome.
　　　　　　　　　　　　　10

相反地，晴朗的天氣，尤其是在冬天，會使人們覺得愉快。當天氣很好的時候，
人們會比較和善，而且比較願意互相幫助。但是當天氣太熱、濕氣太重的時候，
人們可能就比較容易與人發生爭執。

> *in contrast* 相反地
> pleasant ('plɛznt) *adj.* 舒適的；令人愉快的
> willing ('wɪlɪŋ) *adj.* 願意的　　humid ('hjumɪd) *adj.* 潮濕的
> quarrelsome ('kwɔrəlsəm , 'kwɑr-) *adj.* 愛爭吵的

8. (D) 依句意，選 (D) ***sunny*** ('sʌnɪ) *adj.* 晴朗的。而 (A) chilly ('tʃɪlɪ) *adj.*
寒冷的，(B) 多雲的，(C) 下雨的，皆不合句意。

9. (B) ***each other*** 彼此；互相
而 (A)（三者以上）另一個，(C)（二者之中）另一個，(D) 其他別的，
皆不合句意。

10. (B) ***be likely to*** 可能
(A) 喜歡，(C) similarly ('sɪmələ·lɪ) *adv.* 同樣地，不合句意。而 (D)
tend (tɛnd) *v.* 傾向於，tend to「易於；傾向於」，前面不可加 be
動詞，故用法不合。

TEST 34

Read the following passage, and choose the best answer for each blank.

Brisbane, which is the capital of the Australian state of Queensland, has a more relaxed ___1___ than Sydney, perhaps because of its pleasant subtropical climate. Its situation is not as impressive as Sydney's, but the ___2___ which runs through the city center, is full of oceangoing boats, ferries — and small boats as well.

The way of life is probably the most pleasant and relaxed that you will find anywhere in a big city. People usually have large and beautiful gardens so that they can spend their ___3___ outside.

No one needs to ___4___ too much about clothes — it is most comfortable to go around in shorts and without shoes.

While I was in Queensland I often used to relax ___5___ with friends on Brisbane's fantastic beaches — and during the week, too.

1. A. setting
   B. condition
   C. atmosphere
   D. mood

2. A. stream
   B. tunnel
   C. strait
   D. river

3. A. leisure time
   B. rough time
   C. prime time
   D. daylight-saving time

4. A. talk
   B. boast
   C. worry
   D. complain

5. A. at weekends
   B. on festivals
   C. in the evening
   D. in summertime

TEST 34 詳解

Brisbane, *which is the capital of the Australian state of Queens-land,* has a *more* relaxed atmosphere *than Sydney, perhaps because*
$$\underset{1}{}$$
of its pleasant subtropical climate. Its situation is not *as* impressive
as Sydney's, but the river *which runs through the city center,* is
$$\underset{2}{}$$
full of oceangoing boats, ferries — *and* small boats *as well.*.

布里斯本是澳洲昆士蘭省的首府。可能是由於它宜人的亞熱帶氣候，布里斯本的氣氛，要比雪梨來得輕鬆一點。雖然它的位置不如雪梨令人印象深刻，但是流經其市中心的河流，卻充滿了遠洋船隻、渡輪，以及小型汽船。

Brisbane〔'brɪzben, -bən〕n. 布里斯本（澳洲東部海港）
capital〔'kæpətḷ〕n. 首都；首府
Queensland〔'kwinz,lænd, -lənd〕n. 昆士蘭（澳洲東北部一省）
Sydney〔'sɪdnɪ〕n. 雪梨（澳洲首都）
subtropical〔sʌb'trɑpɪkḷ〕adj. 亞熱帶的
impressive〔ɪm'prɛsɪv〕adj. 令人印象深刻的
oceangoing〔'oʃən'goɪŋ〕adj. 航行遠洋的　　ferry〔'fɛrɪ〕n. 渡輪

1. (**C**) (A) setting〔'sɛtɪŋ〕n. 環境
　　　　 (B) condition〔kən'dɪʃən〕n. 情況
　　　　 (C) *atmosphere*〔'ætməs,fɪr〕n. 氣氛
　　　　 (D) mood〔mud〕n. 心情

2. (**D**) 依句意，能夠流經市區，且能航行大型船隻的，應該是「河流」，故選 (D) *river*。而 (A) stream〔strim〕n. 小溪，(B) tunnel〔'tʌnḷ〕n. 隧道，(C) strait〔stret〕n. 海峽，均不合句意。

The way *of life* is *probably* the *most* pleasant and relaxed *that you will find anywhere in a big city.* People *usually* have large and beautiful gardens *so that* they can spend their leisure time outside.

　　那裡的生活方式很可能是所有大城市當中，最令人愉快、最輕鬆的。那裏的人通常都擁有很大而且很漂亮的花園，所以他們空閒時間可以待在戶外。

3. (**A**) (A) *leisure time* 空閒時間
　　(B) rough time 艱苦時期
　　(C) prime time 全盛時期；（電視）黃金時段
　　(D) daylight-saving time 日光節約時間（夏天將時鐘撥快一小時）

No one needs to worry *too much* about clothes — it is *most* comfortable to go *around in shorts and without shoes.*

While I was in Queensland I *often* used to relax *at weekends* with *friends on Brisbane's fantastic beaches — and during the week, too.*

　　大家都不必爲穿著費心 — 可穿著短褲，不穿鞋子到處走，非常地舒適。
　　我在昆士蘭時，常於週末和朋友，在布里斯班迷人的海灘上休息，而且平常的時間也這樣。

4. (**C**) 依句意，「人們不必爲穿著費心」，選 (C) *worry*「擔心」。而 (A) 談話，(B) boast〔bost〕v. 吹牛，(D) complain〔kəm'plen〕v. 抱怨，均不合句意。

5. (**A**) 由 and during the week, too 可知，前面應指「週末」，故選 (A) *at weekends*「週末時」（= *on weekends*）。而 (B) festival〔'fɛstəvḷ〕n. 慶典，(C) 在晚上，(D) summertime〔'sʌmɚ͵taɪm〕n. 夏日，均不合。

TEST 35

Read the following passage, and choose the best answer for each blank.

In recent years, noise pollution, air pollution, and water pollution have become serious problems for city residents. The public is now ___1___ the harm that air and water pollution have done. However, few people recognize the influence noise pollution has on health. In fact, noise pollution is no less ___2___ than air and water pollution. The noises of an average city are ___3___ serious damage to the inhabitants' hearing. For instance, in the United States, one person out of twenty has suffered some hearing loss. And all over the world the situation is getting worse all the time, since noise increases with the population. The experts say that in twenty years the cities will be ___4___ they are today and that it will ___5___ everybody's efforts to keep city noises from increasing.

1. A. complaining
   B. exposing to
   C. aware of
   D. conscious that

2. A. advantageous
   B. harmful
   C. beneficial
   D. blessed

3. A. as loud as to cause
   B. so loud that it causes
   C. loud enough to cause
   D. loud enough that they cause

4. A. twice as noisy as
   B. as twice noisy as
   C. twice as noisily as
   D. as twice noisily as

5. A. make
   B. cost
   C. take
   D. waste

TEST 35 詳解

In recent years, noise pollution, air pollution, ***and*** water pollution have become serious problems *for city residents*. The public
is *now* aware of the harm ***that*** *air and water pollution have done*.
    1

近年來，噪音污染、空氣污染，以及水污染，都已成爲都市居民的嚴重問
題。現在大家都知道空氣污染和水污染所造成的傷害。

    recent (ˈrisn̩t) *adj.* 最近的   resident (ˈrɛzədənt) *n.* 居民

1. (**C**) *be aware of* 知道
    (A) 應改爲 complaining about「抱怨」。
    (B) 應改爲 be exposed to「暴露於～之中；接觸到～」。
    (D) 應改爲 be conscious of「知道」(= *be aware of*)。

However, few people recognize the influence *noise pollution has*
on health. *In fact*, noise pollution is *no less* harmful ***than*** *air and*
                                                          2
water pollution. The noises *of an average city* are loud *enough* to
                                                                    3
cause serious damage *to the inhabitants' hearing*.

然而，很少人注意到噪音污染對健康的影響。事實上，噪音污染的傷害，和空氣
污染及水污染一樣嚴重。一般都市的噪音，甚至大得足以嚴重損害居民的聽力。

    recognize (ˈrɛkəɡˌnaɪz) *v.* 認出；察覺   average (ˈævərɪdʒ) *adj.* 普通的
    inhabitant (ɪnˈhæbətənt) *n.* 居民   *no less ··· than = as ··· as* 和···一樣

2. (**B**) (A) advantageous (ˌædvənˈtedʒəs) *adj.* 有利的
    (B) ***harmful*** (ˈhɑrmfəl) *adj.* 有害的
    (C) beneficial (ˌbɛnəˈfɪʃəl) *adj.* 有益的
    (D) blessed (ˈblɛsɪd) *adj.* 幸福的

3. (**C**) ***loud enough to cause*** ~　聲音大得足以造成~

　　(A) 應改爲 so loud as to cause。　***so ~ as to*** 如此~以致於

　　(B) 由於 noises 爲複數名詞，故應改爲 so loud that ***they*** cause
　　　　才正確。

　　(D) 應改爲 loud enough to cause。

For instance, in the United States, one person *out of twenty* has

suffered some hearing loss. *And all over the world* the situation is

getting worse *all the time,* ***since*** *noise increases with the population.*

The experts say ***that*** *in twenty years the cities will be twice as noisy*

<u>as they are today</u> ***and that*** *it will take everybody's efforts to keep*

city noises from increasing.

例如在美國，每二十人就有一人患有聽力衰退的疾病。在全世界，這種情況愈
來愈嚴重，因爲噪音會隨著人口成長而增加。專家指出，再過二十年，都市裏
的噪音，將會是現在的二倍大。因此，需要大家共同努力，以防止噪音繼續增
加。

　　suffer〔'sʌfə〕*v.* 遭受　　***all the time*** 一直
　　expert〔'ɛkspət〕*n.* 專家

4. (**A**) 倍數的表達法：「倍數＋as＋形容詞或副詞＋as ~」，修飾名詞 the
　　　　cities，須用形容詞，故選 (A) ***twice as noisy as***。

5. (**C**) 依句意，應是某事「需要」大家共同努力，故選 (C) ***take***「需要」。
　　　　其用法爲：「It takes (*sb.*)＋*sth.*＋to V.」。若指人努力去做某事，
　　　　則用「*sb.* makes an effort to V.」。

TEST 36

Read the following passage, and choose the best answer for each blank.

Long before printing was invented, traders would make signs on walls to ___1___ attention to their products. And merchants hung out signs with pictures of boots, or gloves, or whatever they sold, as a way ___2___ information in order to do business. With the coming of printing, and especially the newspaper, advertising ___3___ just being an announcement about something to being an argument and suggestion to make people buy the product. Weekly papers printed in England as early as the 1650's ___4___ coffee, chocolate, and tea. Today, advertising is considered a "science" as well as an art. Research is done; studies are made of consumer tastes and habits and ads are tested and checked, so that there will be the greatest ___5___ the money spent.

1. A. pay
    B. call
    C. receive
    D. call away

2. A. to publishing
    B. for spreading
    C. of spreading
    D. for giving

3. A. started with
    B. proceeded with
    C. resulted from
    D. developed from

4. A. had advertised
    B. had advertising for
    C. had advertisement
    D. had advertised of

5. A. response to
    B. recompense for
    C. return for
    D. reaction on

TEST 36 詳解

Long before printing was invented, traders would make signs

on walls to call attention *to their products*. **And** merchants hung out
$\quad$ 1

signs *with pictures of boots, or gloves, or **whatever** they sold*, *as a*

way *of spreading information* in order to do business.
$\quad\quad$ 2

早在印刷術發明之前,貿易商就在牆上做招牌,以吸引人們注意他們的產品。商人們掛出招牌,這些招牌上有長靴、手套,或任何他們賣的東西的圖片,以作爲散播消息、招攬生意的一種方法。

printing ('prɪntɪŋ) *n.* 印刷   trader ('tredɚ) *n.* 商人
sign (saɪn) *n.* 招牌;告示   merchant ('mɝtʃənt) *n.* 商人

1. (**B**) ***call one's attention to*** 使某人注意
     (A) pay attention to 注意
     (C) receive *one's* attention 受某人注意
     (D) call away attention 引開注意力

2. (**C**) ***a way of V-ing = a way to*** + V. 一種~的方法
     spread (sprɛd) *v.* 散播
     (A) publish ('pʌblɪʃ) *v.* 出版;刊登
     (D) give 爲授與動詞,其用法爲:「give *sth.* to *sb.*」,在此不合。

*With the coming of printing, **and** especially the newspaper*, advertis-

ing developed *from just being an announcement* about something to
$\quad\quad$ 3

being an argument and suggestion to make people buy the product.

Weekly papers *printed in England* *as early* *as the 1650's* had adver-
4

tising *for coffee, chocolate, and tea.*

隨著印刷，尤其是報紙的問世，廣告從僅僅是一份關於某產品的公告，發展成
為促使人們購買該產品的理由或建議。早在一六五〇年代，英國的週報就已刊
登有咖啡、巧克力，以及茶的廣告。

> advertising (ˈædvɚˌtaɪzɪŋ) *n.* 廣告　announcement (əˈnaʊnsmənt) *n.* 公告
> argument (ˈɑrgjəmənt) *n.* 理由；爭論　weekly (ˈwiklɪ) *adj.* 每週的

3. (**D**) 依句意，選 (D) ***develop from ~ to …*** 「由~發展至…」。
　　(A) start with　以~為起始　　　　(B) proceed with　進行；繼續
　　(C) result from　起因於

4. (**B**) ***have advertising for ~*** 有~的廣告
　　advertise 只以人當主詞，故 (A)，(D) 均不合。(C) advertisement 為
　　可數名詞，依句意為複數，且後面需加介系詞 for，故不選。

Today, advertising is considered a "science" *as well as* an art.

Research is done; studies are made *of consumer tastes* *and* habits

and ads are tested and checked, *so that* there will be the greatest

return for the money spent.
5

今天，廣告被視為一門「科學」和一種藝術。廣告商做研究，調查消費者的愛
好和習慣，並測試及考核該廣告的效果，以期使成本能得到最大的回收。

> consumer (kənˈsumɚ) *n.* 消費者　taste (test) *n.* 品味；愛好

5. (**C**) 依句意，應選 (C) ***return for ~*** 「對於~的回報；~的利潤」。
　　而 (A) response to ~「對~的回應」，(B) recompense (ˈrɛkəmˌpɛns)
　　n. 補償，(D) reaction on ~「對~的反應」，均不合句意。

TEST 37

Read the following passage, and choose the best answer for each blank.

One of the traveler's greatest problems in a new city is
___1___ his or her way to those things ___2___ mean survival:
food, a place to ___3___, and medical help. Most cities have
___4___ complicated network of transport ___5___ the visitor's
first task is to master ___6___ transport system. The visitor
should get hold ___7___ a transport map of the city and become
familiar ___8___ the local routes and timetables. Armed with
this knowledge and a good sense of direction, a tourist ___9___
be able to find the way ___10___ any part of the city.

1. A. to be finding
   B. to have found
   C. to find
   D. for finding

2. A. where
   B. which
   C. when
   D. what

3. A. stay
   B. staying
   C. have stayed
   D. be staying

4. A. the
   B. this
   C. that
   D. a

5. A. and
   B. but
   C. as
   D. while

6. A. a
   B. the
   C. one
   D. those

7. A. on
   B. of
   C. to
   D. at

8. A. with
   B. to
   C. in
   D. for

9. A. had
   B. might have
   C. should
   D. could have

10. A. out
    B. over
    C. up
    D. to

TEST 37 詳解

One *of the traveler's greatest problems in a new city* is to find
                                                          1
his or her way to those things *which mean survival*: *food, a place*
                                          2
to stay, *and medical help*. Most cities have a complicated network
    3   4
of transport and the visitor's first task is to master the transport
                   5   6
system.

　　旅客在到達一個新的城市時，所遇到最大的問題之一，就是要找到，那些
所謂可以讓他或她生存的事物：食物、歇腳處，以及醫療救助。大部分的城市
都有複雜的運輸網路，旅客首要的工作，就是要精通這種運輸系統。

　　find one's way to ~ 找到去~的路
　　survival (sə'vaɪvl) *n.* 生存　　medical ('mɛdɪkl̩) *adj.* 醫學的；醫療的
　　complicated ('kɑmplə,ketɪd) *adj.* 複雜的　　network ('nɛt,wɜk) *n.* 網路
　　transport ('trænsport , -port) *n.* 運輸　　master ('mæstɚ , 'mɑs-) *v.* 精通

1. (**C**) 不定詞片語 to find … things 作主詞補語，故選 (C)。
　　而 (A) 表「正在」找到，(B) 表「已經」找到，均不合句意。

2. (**B**) which 為關係代名詞，引導形容詞子句，在子句中，作 mean 的主詞。
　　而 (A) where ，(C) when 分別是表地點與表時間的關係副詞，無法作
　　mean 的主詞，(D) what 為複合關代，不可引導形容詞子句。

3. (**A**) 不定詞 to 之後須接原形動詞，故選 (A)。而 (C) 表完成，(D) 表進行，
　　均不合句意。

4. (**D**) 可數名詞 network 在本文中第一次出現，而且並非指某特定運輸網
　　路，故前面加不定冠詞 a ，而 (A) (B) (C) 均表特定，在此不合。

5. (**A**) 空格前後兩句的句意連貫，故選累積連接詞 (A) **and**「而且」。

　　　(B) 但是，(C) 由於，(D) 當～時候，均不合句意。

6. (**B**) 前面已提過 transport，再次提及時，有特定的意思，故選 (B) **the** 。

The visitor should get hold of a transport map *of the city* and be-
　　　　　　　　　　　　　7

come familiar with the local routes and timetables. *Armed with*
　　　　　　　　8

this knowledge and a good sense of direction, a tourist should be
　　　　　　　　　　　　　　　　　　　　　　　　　　　9

able to find the way *to any part of the city.*
　　　　　　　　10

旅客應該要有一張全市的交通地圖，而且要熟悉當地路線及時刻表。如果觀光
客具備有這樣的知識，以及良好的方向感，就可以找到通往城市任何地方的路。

* Armed with … direction 是由 If he is armed with … direction，
　簡化而來的分詞構句。

　　local〔'lokl〕*adj.* 當地的　　　route〔rut〕*n.* 路線
　　timetable〔'taɪm,tebl〕*n.* 時刻表
　　be armed with 具備　　*a sense of direction* 方向感

7. (**B**) **get hold of** 抓住；擁有 (= *catch hold of*)

8. (**A**) ⎰ **become** ⎱ **familiar with** 熟悉
　　　　　⎱ **be** ⎰

9. (**C**) 空格後出現動詞 be，爲原形動詞，故知空格應填入助動詞 should，
　　　　　選 (C)。而 (A)、(B)、(D) 其後須接過去分詞，且與句意不合。

10. (**D**) **find the way to ~** 找到通往～的路(= *find one's way to ~*)

TEST 38

Read the following passage, and choose the best answer for each blank.

Stamp collecting is one of the most popular hobbies of all time. It is a hobby ___1___ by the rich and the poor ___2___, because it costs as much as you want ___3___ cost. It may cost very ___4___ if that's all you can afford. And a young person can have as much fun ___5___ it as an adult.

How do you begin a stamp collection? In a stamp dealer's shop, a bookstore or your local post office, you will find stamp collecting kits. These kits contain ___6___ you need to begin your collection.

___7___ you have begun collecting, save ___8___ on the mail that comes to your home. Ask friends to save canceled stamps ___9___ you. Find friends who share your hobby and ___10___ stamps with them.

1. A. owned
   B. shared
   C. owning
   D. sharing

2. A. alike
   B. similar
   C. same
   D. like

3. A. it to
   B. it
   C. to
   D. that

4. A. small
   B. tiny
   C. less
   D. little

5. A. to
   B. on
   C. with
   D. for

6. A. those
   B. what
   C. which
   D. that

7. A. Soon
   B. Right
   C. Then
   D. Once

8. A. the stamps
   B. the stamp
   C. a stamp
   D. stamps

9. A. about
   B. for
   C. to
   D. toward

10. A. take
    B. send
    C. trade
    D. give

TEST 38 詳解

Stamp collecting is one *of the most popular hobbies of all*

time. It is a hobby *shared by the rich and the poor alike*, *because*
　　　　　　　　　　　　　1　　　　　　　　　　　　　　　2

it costs as much **as** *you want it to cost*. It may cost *very little if*
　　　　　　　　　　　3　　　　　　　　　　　　　　　　4

that's all you can afford. **And** a young person can have *as* much

fun with it **as an adult**.
　　　5

集郵一直是人們最喜愛的嗜好之一。不論貧富,都一樣可以享有這種嗜好,
因為你想花多少錢集郵都可以。如果你能負擔的錢不多,那也就不用花太多錢。
而年輕人也能和成年人一樣,從其中得到一樣多的樂趣。

> **stamp collecting** 集郵　　**of all time** 自古以來
> afford〔ə'fɔrd〕v. 負擔得起　　adult〔ə'dʌlt〕n. 成人

1. (**B**) shared by … alike 為過去分詞片語,是由形容詞子句 which is
shared … alike 簡化而來。　　share〔ʃɛr〕v. 分享;共有

2. (**A**) A *and* B *alike* = *both* A *and* B 「A 和 B 二者都…」,此處的
alike 為副詞,而 (B)(C)(D) 均非副詞,故不可選。

3. (**A**) want *sth*. to V. 中,to 不可省略,故選 (A) *it to* 。而 you want it
to cost = you want to spend,因「事物 + cost」而「人 + spend」。

4. (**D**) 依句意,指「錢」的花費,而 money 為不可數名詞,故選 (D) *little* 。
而 (A) small 「小的」,(B) tiny〔'taɪnɪ〕*adj.* 微小的,與句意不合。
(C) less 為比較級,之前不可用 very 修飾,故不可選。

5. (**C**) *have fun with* ~ 玩~玩得很開心

How do you begin a stamp collection? *In a stamp dealer's shop,*

a bookstore or your local post office, you will find stamp collecting

kits. These kits contain ***what*** *you need to begin your collection.*
　　　　　　　　　　　　　6

　　你要如何開始集郵？在販賣郵票的商店、書店，或你家當地的郵局，都可
以找到集郵的用品。這些用品包含了你開始集郵所需要的一切東西。

　　　dealer〔'dilɚ〕*n.* 商人　　local〔'lokḷ〕*adj.* 當地的　　kit〔kɪt〕*n.* 成套用品

6. (**B**) 依句意，空格需填一個關係代名詞，且應為先行詞兼作關代之複合關
　　　　代，故選 (B) ***what*** (= *those which* = *the things which*)。

Once *you have begun collecting,* save the stamps *on the mail*
　7　　　　　　　　　　　　　　　　　8

that comes to your home. Ask friends to save canceled stamps *for*
　　　　　　　　　　　　　　　　　　　　　　　　　　　　　　9

you. Find friends *who share your hobby* ***and*** trade stamps *with them.*
　　　　　　　　　　　　　　　　　　　　　　10

　　一旦開始集郵，就把寄到你家的信件上的郵票都留下來。同時也請朋友替
你留下用過的郵票。也可以找一些有同樣嗜好的朋友，一起來交換郵票。

　　canceled stamp 蓋過郵戳的郵票

7. (**D**) 空格需填一個從屬連接詞，且依句意，選 (D) ***Once***「一旦」。

8. (**A**) 特指在郵件上的郵票，要加定冠詞 the，且依句意，mail「郵件」
　　　　（集合名詞）上的郵票應不只一張，故 stamp 須用複數形，選 (A)。

9. (**B**) ***save*** *sth.* ***for*** *sb.* 為某人保留某物

10. (**C**) ***trade*** *sth.* ***with*** *sb.* 與某人交換某物 (= *exchange sth. with sb.*)

TEST 39

Read the following passage, and choose the best answer for each blank.

One of the most urgent problems in teaching handwriting is presented by the left-handed child. The ___1___ policy has been to attempt to induce all children to write with their right hands. Parents and teachers alike have an antipathy ___2___ the children's using their left hands. ___3___, psychologists have shown beyond a doubt that some people are naturally left-handed and that it is much ___4___ difficult for them to do any skillful act with the right hand than with the left hand. Some believe, ___5___, that to compel left-handed children to write with their right hands may ___6___ them nervous and may cause stammering. ___7___ seem to be some cases in which this is true, ___8___ in the majority of children who change over, no ill effects are noticed. ___9___ these difficulties, left-handedness sometimes seems to cause mirror writing — writing from right to left — and reversals in reading, as reading "was" for " ___10___ ."

1. A. traditional
   B. revolutionary
   C. obedient
   D. complicated

2. A. for
   B. by
   C. to
   D. from

3. A. On the other hand
    B. On the contrary
    C. As a consequence
    D. For instance

4. A. too
    B. more
    C. so
    D. far

5. A. however
    B. strange to say
    C. furthermore
    D. to the contrary

6. A. let
    B. cause
    C. bring
    D. make

7. A. It
    B. There
    C. They
    D. Those

8. A. unless
    B. although
    C. because
    D. if

9. A. In spite of
    B. Far from
    C. Judging from
    D. In addition to

10. A. saw
    B. war
    C. sew
    D. wax

TEST 39 詳解

One *of the most urgent problems in teaching handwriting* is presented *by the left-handed child*. The <u>traditional</u> policy has been
₁
to attempt to induce all children to write *with their right hands*.

Parents and teachers *alike* have an antipathy *to the children's using*
₂

their left hands.

在教寫字時，最迫切的問題之一，是出現在左撇子的小孩身上。傳統的政策向來是，試著引導所有的小朋友用右手寫字。父母和老師都一樣，不喜歡孩子使用左手。

> urgent〔ˈɝdʒənt〕*adj.* 迫切的
> handwriting〔ˈhændˌraɪtɪŋ〕*n.* 書寫方法；筆跡
> present〔prɪˈzɛnt〕*v.* 出現；呈現
> left-handed〔ˈlɛftˈhændɪd〕*adj.* 慣用左手的　attempt〔əˈtɛmpt〕*v.* 企圖
> induce〔ɪnˈdjus〕*v.* 引誘；引導　alike〔əˈlaɪk〕*adj.* 同樣的
> antipathy〔ænˈtɪpəθɪ〕*n.* 反感；憎惡

1. (**A**) (A) *traditional*〔trəˈdɪʃənḷ〕*adj.* 傳統的
   (B) revolutionary〔ˌrɛvəˈluʃənˌɛrɪ〕*adj.* 革命的
   (C) obedient〔əˈbidɪənt〕*adj.* 服從的
   (D) complicated〔ˈkɑmpləˌketɪd〕*adj.* 複雜的

2. (**C**) *have an antipathy to ~* 不喜歡~；對~有反感

On the other hand, psychologists have shown *beyond a doubt* **that**
　　　　3

some people are naturally left-handed **and that** *it is much more dif-*
　　　　　　　　　　　　　　　　　　　　　　　　　4

ficult for them to do any skillful act with the right hand **than** *with*

the left hand. Some believe, *furthermore*, **that** *to compel left-handed*
　　　　　　　　　　　　　　　　5

children to write with their right hands may make them nervous
　　　　　　　　　　　　　　　　　　　　6

and *may cause stammering.*

但另一方面，心理學家已經證實，有些人天生就是慣用左手，而且對他們來說，
用右手做任何需要技巧的動作，比用左手做困難得多。此外，有些人認為，強
迫左撇子的小孩用右手寫字，可能會使他們緊張，並且可能導致口吃的毛病。

　　psychologist〔saɪˋkɑlədʒɪst〕*n.* 心理學家
　　beyond a doubt 無疑地
　　compel〔kʌmˋpɛl〕*v.* 強迫
　　stammering〔ˋstæmərɪŋ〕*n.* 口吃；結巴

3. (**A**) 依句意，選 (A) ***on the other hand*** 另一方面。
　　　而 (B) on the contrary「相反地」，(C) as a consequence「因此」，
　　　(D) for instance「例如」，均不合句意。

4. (**B**) 由連接詞 than 可知，此處須用比較級，故選 (B) ***more***。

5. (**C**) 依句意，選 (C) ***furthermore*** 「此外」。

　　　而 (A) however 「然而」，(B) strange to say 「說來奇怪」，
　　　(D) to the contrary 「相反的」，均不合句意。

6. (**D**) 依句意，「使」他們緊張，且受詞補語為形容詞，故選 (D) ***make***。

　　　而 (A) let 為使役動詞，接受詞後須接原形動詞，(B) cause 「導致」，
　　　接受詞後須接不定詞 to-V；而 (C) bring 「帶來」，則與句意不合。

<u>There</u> seem to be some cases *in **which** this is true,* |*although* in
7　　　　　　　　　　　　　　　　　　　　　　　　　　8

*the majority of children **who** change over,* no ill effects are noticed.

<u>*In addition to* these difficulties</u>, left-handedness *sometimes* seems to
　　　　9

cause mirror writing—*writing from right to left*—***and*** reversals *in*

reading, as reading "was" for "saw."
　　　　　　　　　　　　10

似乎有些個案顯示這種說法是對的，雖然在大多數已改變寫字習慣的兒童當
中，並沒有發現有不良的影響。除了這些困難之外，慣用左手的習慣，有時似
乎也會導致相反的書寫方法——由右寫到左，以及顛倒的閱讀法，如把 "was"
看成 "saw"。

　　　majority〔mə`dʒɔrətɪ〕*n.* 大多數　　***change over*** 改變
　　　mirror writing 反寫的書寫方法　　reversal〔rɪ`vɝsəl, sl〕*n.* 顛倒

7. (**B**) 表示「有～」要用「there + be 動詞」的形式，故選 (B)。

8. (**B**)　依句意，選 (B) *although* 「雖然」。而 (A) unless 「除非」，
　　　　(C) because 「因為」，(D) if 「如果」，均不合。

9. (**D**)　*in addition to* ~　除了~之外
　　　　(A) in spite of 僅管　　　　(B) far from 一點也不
　　　　(C) judging from ~　由~判斷

10. (**A**)　依句意，"was" 由右寫到左，就變成 "saw"，故選 (A)。

TEST 40

Read the following passage, and choose the best answer for each blank.

I cannot help wondering about the effect of TV on the health of the present-day children, many of ___1___ spend more than two or three hours a day watching TV. It may be a pleasant entertainment for them, and in the entertainment they may ___2___ some useful instruction.

But they are being deprived ___3___ the exercise which they would otherwise have, ___4___ for their growing bodies and for their powers of ___5___ and imagination. The more they watch TV, the more ___6___ they become. Further, all this ___7___ on TV must be tiring to the eyes and the nerves of the children. It is not natural for people to spend a long time in front of a flickering ___8___. Even if their eyes get accustomed to ___9___, maybe with the help of spectacles, their nerves are sure to suffer ___10___.

1. A. them
   B. those
   C. whom
   D. children

2. A. receive
   B. grant
   C. accept
   D. confess

3. A. by
   B. of
   C. for
   D. through

4. A. either
   B. not merely
   C. both
   D. instead of

5. A. illusion
   B. authority
   C. hesitation
   D. creativity

6. A. passive
   B. original
   C. vivid
   D. optimistic

7. A. emphasis
   B. reliance
   C. influence
   D. concentration

8. A. cinema
   B. spotlight
   C. mirage
   D. screen

9. A. those
   B. it
   C. themselves
   D. either of them

10. A. in full swing
    B. to the slightest degree
    C. in the long run
    D. from bad to worse

TEST 40 詳解

I cannot help wondering about the effect *of TV* on the health of the present-day children, *many of* **whom** *spend more than two or*
<u>1</u>
three hours a day watching TV. It may be a pleasant entertainment for them, ***and*** *in the entertainment* they may receive some useful
<u>2</u>
instruction.

我忍不住想知道，電視對現代兒童的健康，會造成什麼樣的影響。許多兒童每天看電視的時間，都超過兩三個小時。電視或許是種令兒童喜愛的娛樂，藉由這種娛樂方式，他們可以得到有用的知識。

> ***cannot help + V-ing*** 不得不；忍不住
> instruction〔ɪnˋstrʌkʃən〕*n.* 指導；知識

1. (**C**) 關係代名詞 whom 引導形容詞子句，修飾 children。在子句中 whom 作 of 的受詞，所以是受格。

2. (**A**) 依句意，選 (A) ***receive***〔rɪˋsiv〕*v.* 收到；得到。
    而 (C) accept〔əkˋsɛpt〕*v.* 接受，則著重以「愉悅的態度」或是「由自己去爭取來」而得到、取得之事實，如：
    I received an invitation from them, but I didn't accept it.
    （我收到他們的邀請，但並未接受。）
    而 (B) grant〔grænt〕*v.* 答應，(D) confess〔kənˋfɛs〕*v.* 承認，則不合句意。

But they are being deprived of the exercise *which they would*
　　　　　　　　　　　　　　　3

otherwise have, both *for their growing bodies* **and** *for their powers*
　　　　　　　　　4

of creativity and imagination. The more they watch TV, the
　　5

more passive they become.
　　6

　　但是電視剝奪了他們原本可經由其他方式可獲得的 —— 有益身心成長的運動，以及運用創造力與想像力的機會。電視看得愈多，他們也就變得愈被動。

　　otherwise〔'ʌðə‚waɪz〕*adv.* 以其他方式

3. (**B**) *be deprived of* ~ 被剝奪～

4. (**C**) ***both*** A ***and*** B A 與 B
　　(A) either 須與 or 連用。　　　either A or B 不是 A 就是 B
　　(B) not merely (= *not only*) 須與 but (also) 連用。
　　　　not merely A but (also) B 不僅 A 而且 B
　　(D) instead of ~「而不是～」，不合句意。

5. (**D**) ***creativity*** 〔‚krie'tɪvətɪ〕*n.* 創造力
　　(A) illusion〔ɪ'ljuʒən〕*n.* 幻覺　　(B) authority〔ə'θɔrətɪ〕*n.* 權威
　　(C) hesitation〔‚hɛzə'teʃən〕*n.* 猶豫

6. (**A**) ***passive*** 〔'pæsɪv〕*adj.* 被動的
　　(B) original〔ə'rɪdʒənḷ〕*adj.* 原本的；最初的
　　(C) vivid〔'vɪvɪd〕*adj.* 生動的
　　(D) optimistic〔‚ɑptə'mɪstɪk〕*adj.* 樂觀的

Further, all this <u>concentration</u> *on TV* must be tiring to the eyes
                              7

and the nerves *of the children.* It is not natural *for people* to spend

a long time *in front of a flickering* <u>screen</u>. ***Even if*** their eyes get
                                              8

accustomed to <u>it</u>, *maybe with the help* *of spectacles*, their nerves
               9

are sure to suffer *in the long run*.
                    10

此外，如此專注於電視，兒童的眼睛和神經，都會覺得十分疲倦。長時間看著閃爍不定的螢幕，對人而言，是種不自然的現象。即使可以藉由眼鏡的幫助，使眼睛習慣這種現象，到最後神經方面必定會受損害。

further〔'fɜðɚ〕*adv.* 此外　　nerve〔nɜv〕*n.* 神經
flickering〔'flɪkərɪŋ〕*adj.* 閃爍不定的　　***get accustomed to*** 習慣於
spectacles〔'spɛktəkḷz〕*n. pl.* 眼鏡

7. (**D**) *concentration*〔͵kɑnsṇ'treʃən〕*n.* 專心
　　(A) emphasis〔'ɛmfəsɪs〕*n.* 強調
　　(B) reliance〔rɪ'laɪəns〕*n.* 依賴
　　(C) influence〔'ɪnfluəns〕*n.* 影響

8. (**D**) *screen*〔skrin〕*n.* 螢幕
　　(A) cinema〔'sɪnəmə〕*n.* 電影
　　(B) spotlight〔'spɑt͵laɪt〕*n.* 聚光燈
　　(C) mirage〔mə'rɑʒ〕*n.* 海市蜃樓

9. (**B**) 依句意，空格應填代名詞 it，代替不定詞片語 to spend a long time
… screen 。

10. (**C**) ***in the long run*** 到最後
　　　　(A) in full swing 在最熱烈的時候
　　　　(B) to the slightest degree 到最輕微的程度
　　　　(D) from bad to worse 每下愈況；愈來愈糟

TEST 41

Read the following passage, and choose the best answer for each blank.

A young man had become friends with a fellow student who was blind. For the first time, he became aware ___1___ the problems faced by those who can not ___2___. To experience those problems ___3___, he taped his eyes shut, put on dark glasses, picked up a white cane, and went out into the ___4___ world. Perhaps it was a foolish thing to do, for ___5___ a blind person does not venture out without ___6___ training first. However, he survived the day ___7___ the help of many kindly people who offered help ___8___ the way. ___9___ was a day that he would not soon forget, for it was not easy to ___10___ the activities of the busy city.

1. A. to
   B. with
   C. of
   D. on

2. A. hear
   B. see
   C. smell
   D. taste

3. A. firsthand
   B. secondhand
   C. at hand
   D. off hand

4. A. seeing
   B. seen
   C. sight
   D. saw

5. A. almost
   B. even
   C. hardly
   D. nearly

6. A. a good deal of
   B. a good number of
   C. lot of
   D. large amount of

7. A. with
   B. without
   C. under
   D. in

8. A. in
   B. by
   C. around
   D. along

9. A. It
   B. Such
   C. What
   D. That

10. A. deal in
    B. handle with
    C. cope with
    D. dealing with

TEST 41 詳解

A young man had become friends *with a fellow student **who** was*

blind. For the first time, he became aware <u>of</u> the problems *faced*
　　　　　　　　　　　　　　　　　　　　　1

*by those **who** can not <u>see</u>. To experience those problems <u>firsthand</u>*, he
　　　　　　　　　　2　　　　　　　　　　　　　　　　　3

taped his eyes shut, put on dark glasses, picked up a white cane,

and went out into the <u>seeing</u> world.
　　　　　　　　　　　4

　　有位年輕人和一位眼盲的同學成爲好朋友。他生平第一次開始察覺到盲人
所面對的問題。爲了要直接體驗這些問題,他把眼睛矇起來,戴上墨鏡,拿了
一枝白手杖,就走到這個看得見的世界。

　　fellow〔ˈfɛlo〕*adj.* 同類的　　face〔fes〕*v.* 面對
　　tape sth. shut 把某物貼住
　　put on 戴上　　***dark glasses*** 墨鏡
　　pick up 拿起　　cane〔ken〕*n.* 手杖

1. (**C**)　***be / become aware of*** 知道;察覺到

2. (**B**)　依句意,他意識到眼睛「看」不見的人所面對的問題,故選 (B) ***see***。
　　　　而 (A) 聽到,(C) 聞起來,(D) 嚐起來,均不合句意。

3. (**A**)　以句意,他要「直接」體驗這些問題,故選 (A) ***firsthand***「直接;第一
　　　　手地」。而 (B) secondhand「間接地;第二手地」,(C) at hand
　　　　「在手邊」,(D) off hand「馬上;立刻」,均不合。

4. (**A**)　依上下文,走到「看得見的」世界,故選 (A) ***seeing***〔ˈsiɪŋ〕*adj.* 看得
　　　　見的。

Perhaps it was a foolish thing to do, *for* <u>even</u> a blind person does
             5

not venture out without <u>a good of deal</u> training first. *However*, he
           6

survived the day <u>*with*</u> the help of many kindly people *who* offered help
       -7-

<u>along the way</u>. <u>It</u> was a day *that* he would not soon forget, *for it*
  8   9

was not easy to <u>cope with</u> the activities <u>of</u> the busy city.
       10

也許這是一件很蠢的事，因為即使是盲人，如果沒有先經過一番訓練，是不會冒險出門的。然而那一天，他竟然毫髮無傷，因為沿途一直有許多好心人士的幫忙。而這一天也令他難以忘懷，因為要應付繁忙城市裡的活動，並不是一件容易的事。

  venture〔ˈvɛntʃɚ〕*v.* 冒險 survive〔səˈvaɪv〕*v.* 自～中生還
  kindly〔ˈkaɪndlɪ〕*adj.* 親切的；仁慈的

5. (**B**) 依句意，「即使」是盲人也要經過訓練，故選 (B) *even*「即使」。而 (A)
    almost「幾乎」，(C) hardly「幾乎不」，(D) nearly「幾乎」，均不合。

6. (**A**) *a good deal of training* 大量的訓練
    而 (B) a good number of「很多的～」是用來修飾「可數名詞」，
    而 training「訓練」是不可數名詞，故 (B) 不合。(C) 和 (D) 均可用來
    修飾不可數名詞，但是 (C) 要改成 lots of 或 a lot of，(D)則要改
    成 a large amount of，故不選。

7. (**A**) 依句意，那天「有」許多好心人士幫忙，故介系詞用 *with*，選 (A)。

8. (**D**) 依句意，應是「沿」途都有人幫忙，故選 (D) *along*「沿著」。

9. (**A**) 用代名詞 It 來代表「那一天」，故選 (A)。

10. (**C**) 空格須填原形動詞，且依句意，選 (C) *cope with*「應付」。而 (A) deal
    in「做～的買賣」，不合句意。(B) handle〔ˈhændl〕*v.* 處理，為及物
    動詞，不需加介系詞，而 (D) 須改成原形動詞 deal with「處理」。

TEST 42

Read the following passage, and choose the best answer for each blank.

Hans Christian Anderson (1805-1875) is probably ___1___ writer of fairy tales in the world. He was born ___2___ a very poor family in Denmark. He was an only child. His father was a free-thinking man who ___3___ the mind of his son. He read him stories and plays, showed him nature's beauty, and made toys ___4___ young Hans. Hans was eleven years old when his father ___5___ .

Hans showed ___6___ in the arts — writing, painting, singing, and acting. He was also a dreamer. At 17, Hans was ___7___ to school by some of his older friends, in order to develop his talent and get the education he ___8___ . This was a difficult period in his life but he ___9___ his studies. ___10___ that he started to write. When he died, he had written some 156 tales.

1. A. well known
   B. best known
   C. the best known
   D. better known

2. A. by
   B. into
   C. at
   D. on

3. A. tried opening
   B. tried to open
   C. trying to open
   D. tries opening

4. A. to
   B. for
   C. by
   D. of

5. A. dies
   B. dead
   C. has been dead
   D. died

6. A. a great interest
   B. was interested
   C. greatly interested
   D. interest great

7. A. sent
   B. entered
   C. went
   D. enrolled

8. A. has missed
   B. missed
   C. missing
   D. had missed

9. A. succeeded to
   B. succeeded in
   C. successful in
   D. succeeded

10. A. By
    B. After
    C. In
    D. At

TEST 42 詳解

Hans Christian Anderson (1805-1875) is *probably* the best
1

known writer *of fairy tales in the world.* He was born into a
2

very poor family *in Denmark.* He was an only child. His father

was a free-thinking man *who tried to open the mind of his son.*
3

He read him stories and plays, showed him nature's beauty, *and*

made toys *for young Hans.* Hans was eleven years old *when his*
4

father died.
5

漢斯‧克里斯昂‧安徒生（1805-1875）大概是全世界最有名的童話故事作家。他出生於丹麥一戶非常貧窮的人家，是家裡唯一的小孩。他的父親思想非常開放，想要啓發他兒子的心靈，所以會唸故事及劇本給兒子聽，並帶他見識大自然的美麗，而且還做玩具給小漢斯玩。漢斯的父親死的時候，他才十一歲。

fairy〔'fɛrɪ〕*adj.* 小神仙的　　*fairy tales* 童話故事；神話故事
free-thinking〔'fri'θɪŋkɪŋ〕*adj.* 思想開放的　　play〔ple〕*n.* 劇本

1. (**C**) well known「有名的」，但依句意爲最高級，故選 (C) *the best known*。

2. (**B**) *be born into*～ 生於～

3. (**B**) 依句意，他「企圖要」開啓他兒子的心靈，因此須用「try + to V.」，且依句意爲過去式，故選 (B)。而 (A)「try + V-ing」則表「試驗～」。

4. (**B**) 他「爲」小漢斯做玩具，表「爲了～」，介系詞用 *for*，選 (B)。

5. (**D**) 人「死亡」，是瞬間的動作，且依句意爲過去式，故選 (D) *died*。

Hans showed <u>a great interest</u> *in the arts — writing, painting,*
　　　　　　　　　6

singing, and acting. He was *also* a dreamer. *At 17,* Hans was <u>sent</u>
　　　　　　　　　　　　　　　　　　　　　　　　　　　　　　　　7

to school *by some of his older friends, in order to develop his talent*

and get the education he had <u>missed</u>. This was a difficult period *in*
　　　　　　　　　　　　　　　　8

*his life **but*** he <u>succeeded</u> *in his studies.* *After that* he started to write.
　　　　　　　　　9　　　　　　　　　　　　10

When he died, he had written some 156 tales.

　　　漢斯對於藝術，如寫作、繪畫、歌唱及表演方面，都展現了極大的興趣。此外，他還是個夢想家。十七歲時，有些較年長的朋友送漢斯去學校讀書，目的就是要培養他的才能，並將他之前錯過的教育補回來。這是他生命中一段艱苦的時期，不過他還是成功地完成學業。之後，他就開始寫作。在他去世時，他已寫了大約一百五十六個故事了。

　　　　acting〔ˋæktɪŋ〕*n.* 表演（藝術）　　　talent〔ˋtælənt〕*n.* 才能
　　　　studies〔ˋstʌdɪz〕*n. pl.* 學業　　some〔sʌm〕*adj.* 大約

6. (**A**) *show a great interest in* 對～很有興趣

7 (**A**) 依句意，他被一些較年長的朋友「送」去上學，故選 (A) *sent*。
　　　　而 (B) enter a school 「入學」，(C) go to school「上學」，
　　　　(D) enroll〔ɪnˋrol〕*v.* 登記；註冊，則不合句意。

8. (**D**) 要將他「之前錯過的」教育補回來，表過去某個定點時間之前完成
　　　　的動作，須用「過去完成式」，故選 (D) *had missed*。

9. (**B**) *succeed in～*「在～方面很成功」。而 (C) 須改為 was successful
　　　　in。

10. (**B**) 完成學業「後」，他才開始寫作，故選 (B) *after*。

TEST 43

Read the following passage, and choose the best answer for each blank.

Only some types of body language, such as posture and certain ___1___ expressions, are universal; ___2___ types are not. For ___3___ , many specific gestures are interpreted ___4___ in different cultures. People in the United States, Canada, and ___5___ of Western Europe nod to signal "yes"; but people in Turkey signal "yes" by ___6___ the head from side to side — in a motion that we might interpret ___7___ "No." And when we ___8___ an O with the thumb and index finger, we mean "OK." But in many Mediterranean countries, this sign means "zero." In Japan, it means "money." And in Tunisia, it means "I'll kill you!" Smart travelers learn ___9___ the spoken and unspoken language of the countries ___10___ .

1. A. face
   B. facing
   C. facial
   D. faces

2. A. another
   B. the other
   C. the others
   D. other

3. A. example
   B. examples
   C. an example
   D. the example

4. A. different
   B. differently
   C. difference
   D. differences

5. A. many
   B. much
   C. every
   D. each

6. A. moving
   B. holding
   C. counting
   D. knocking

7. A. with
   B. as
   C. by
   D. like

8. A. inform
   B. transform
   C. form
   D. reform

9. A. all
   B. some
   C. both
   D. either

10. A. he visits
    B. one visits
    C. they visit
    D. visiting

TEST 43 詳解

Only some types *of body language, such as posture and certain*
　　　　　核心主詞
facial expressions, are universal; other types are not. *For example*,
　1　　　　　動詞　　　　　　　2　　　　　　　　　3
many specific gestures are interpreted *differently in different*
　　　　　　　　　　　　　　　　　　4
cultures. People *in the United States, Canada, **and** much of Western*
　　　　　　　　　　　　　　　　　　　　　　　5
Europe nod to signal "yes"; ***but*** people *in Turkey* signal "yes" *by*
moving the head from side to side — *in a motion **that** we might*
　6
interpret *as* "No."
　7

　　只有一些型式的肢體語言,像是身體姿勢,或某些臉部表情,是全世界共
通的;而另一些就不是了。例如,許多特定的動作,在不同文化中,有不同的
解讀方式。美國、加拿大,以及大多數西歐的人,都以點頭來表示「同意」;但
土耳其人,則用搖頭來表示贊同,而搖頭這個動作我們可能會解讀為「拒絕」。

> ***body language*** 肢體語言　　posture ('pɑstʃɚ) *n.* 姿勢
> expression (ɪk'sprɛʃən) *n.* 表情
> universal (ˌjunə'vɝsḷ) *adj.* 全世界的;共通的
> specific (spɪ'sɪfɪk) *adj.* 特定的　　gesture ('dʒɛstʃɚ) *n.* 姿勢
> interpret (ɪn'tɝprɪt) *v.* 解釋　　nod (nɑd) *v.* 點頭
> signal ('sɪgnḷ) *v.* 表示　　motion ('moʃən) *n.* 動作

1. (**C**) 依句意,選 (C) *facial* ('feʃəl) *adj.* 臉部的。
   facial expressions 臉部表情

2. (**D**) *some types*…; *other types*… 有些形式…;而另一些形式…
   而 (A) another「(三者以上)另一個」須接單數名詞,(B) the other
   「(兩者中的)另一個」,(C) the others「其他的人或物」,為代名詞,
   在此不合。

3. (**A**) *for example* 例如

4. (**B**) 修飾動詞 interpreted，須用副詞，故選 (B) *differently*「不同地」。

5. (**B**) Europe「歐洲」，爲不可數名詞，故用 much 修飾，選 (B)。

6. (**A**) 由下一句「這個動作是我們表示拒絕的動作」可知，空格應填「搖」頭，故選 (A) *move* (muv) *v.* 移動。而 (B) hold「握住」，(C) count「數」，(D) knock「敲」，均不合。

7. (**B**) 依句意，搖頭被我們解讀「爲」拒絕，故選 (B) *as*「作爲」。

And when we *form* an O *with the thumb **and** index finger*, we
　　　　　　8 ↑

mean "O.K." *But in many Mediterranean countries*, this sign means

"zero." *In Japan*, it means "money." *And in Tunisia*, it means "I'll

kill you!" Smart travelers learn <u>both</u> the spoken and unspoken
　　　　　　　　　　　　　　　　　9

language *of the countries* *they visit*.
　　　　　　　　　　　　10

當我們用大姆指和食指作成一個 " O " 形，就表示「沒問題」。不過在一些地中海地區的國家，這個手勢代表「零」。在日本，這代表「錢」。在突尼西亞，這代表「我要殺了你！」。所以聰明的旅客到其他國家旅遊時，會同時學習當地口語，以及非口語的語言。

thumb (θʌm) *n.* 大拇指　　*index finger* 食指
Mediterranean (ˌmɛdətəˈrenɪən) *adj.* 地中海沿岸地區的
Tunisia (tjuˈnɪʃɪən) *n.* 突尼西亞　　*spoken language* 口語

8. (**C**) 依句意，用大姆指和食指「形成」O形，故選 (C) *form* (fɔrm) *v.* 形成。而 (A) inform (ɪnˈfɔrm) *v.* 通知，(B) transform (trænsˈfɔrm) *v.* 轉變，(D) reform (rɪˈfɔrm) *v.* 改革，均不合。

9. (**C**) *both* A *and* B　A 和 B 兩者

10. (**C**) 原句爲 the countries which they visit，which 爲受格，可省略，故選 (C)。

TEST 44

Read the following passage, and choose the best answer for each blank.

Telecommunications companies constantly create new products that help us ___1___ friends and family wherever we may go. Pagers and cellular phones are two forms of new technology that are especially ___2___ with teenagers. Pagers let you receive phone calls by ___3___ the telephone number of the caller. A cellular phone, also ___4___ a cell phone, is a phone you ___5___ and carry in your purse or pocket. Pagers and cellular phones work like regular phones, ___6___ they don't require telephone wires. They are based ___7___ a relatively new technology called wireless communications. ___8___ how they work, it is both a ___9___ symbol ___10___ practical to carry a cell phone or a pager.

1. A. keep up with
   B. keep an eye on
   C. keep away from
   D. keep in touch with

2. A. common
   B. popular
   C. familiar
   D. satisfied

3. A. peeling
   B. pressing
   C. recording
   D. sounding

4. A. we know as
   B. as we know
   C. known as
   D. known for

5. A. pick up
　 B. put up
　 C. line up
　 D. make up

6. A. because
　 B. except
　 C. besides
　 D. therefore

7. A. in
　 B. by
　 C. with
　 D. on

8. A. Whether
　 B. Despite
　 C. Regardless of
　 D. In spite of

9. A. status
　 B. statue
　 C. stature
　 D. statute

10. A. but also
　　 B. and
　　 C. yet
　　 D. as

TEST 44 詳解

Telecommunications companies *constantly* create new products
that help us keep in touch with friends and family **wherever** we
　　　　　　　　　1
may go.

　　電信公司經常會發明新產品，幫助我們無論到那裡，都能和朋友、家人聯
繫。

> telecommunications (ˌtɛləkəˌmjunəˈkeʃənz) *n. pl.* 電信
> constantly (ˈkɑnstəntlɪ) *adv.* 經常地
> create (krɪˈet) *v.* 創造
> product (ˈprɑdəkt) *n.* 產品

1. (**D**) 這些產品能幫助我們和朋友、家人「聯繫」，故選 (D) *keep in
   touch with*「與～聯絡」。
   (A) keep up with 趕上
   (B) keep an eye on 注意
   (C) keep away from 遠離

Pagers and cellular phones are two forms *of new technology* that
are especially *popular* with teenagers. Pagers let you receive phone
　　　　　　　　　2
calls *by recording the telephone number of the caller.* A cellular
　　　　　　3
phone, *also known as* a cell phone, is a phone *you pick up and*
　　　　　　4　　　　　　　　　　　　　　　　　　5
carry in your purse or pocket.

呼叫器和大哥大，就是兩款在青少年間特別流行的新科技。呼叫器能藉由記錄來電者的電話號碼，讓你接到電話。大哥大，又稱為 cell phone，就是可以拿起來，放到皮包或口袋中的電話。

> pager〔'pedʒɚ〕*n.* 呼叫器（ = *beeper*〔'bipɚ〕*n.* ）
> cellular〔'sɛljələ〕*adj.* 許多小單位組成的；細胞的
> ***cellular phone*** 大哥大（ = *cell phone* ）
> teenager〔'tin,edʒɚ〕*n.* 青少年
> purse〔pɜs〕*n.* 錢包　　pocket〔'pakɪt〕*n.* 口袋

2. (**B**) 這些產品在青少年間特別「流行」，故選 (B) ***popular*** 。
　　(A) common〔'kɑmən〕*adj.* 普通的
　　(C) familiar〔fə'mɪljɚ〕*adj.* 熟悉的
　　(D) satisfied〔'sætɪs,faɪd〕*adj.* 滿意的

3. (**C**) 依句意，呼叫器可以「記錄」對方的電話號碼，故選 (C) ***recording*** 。
　　而 (A) peel〔pil〕*v.* 剝（皮），(B) press〔prɛs〕*v.* 壓，(D) sound〔saʊnd〕*v.* 聽起來，均不合句意。

4. (**C**) ***be known as***（ + 身份、名稱 ）「以～（ 身份、名稱 ）著稱」，空格前面省略 which is，故選 (C) ***known as*** 。
　　(B) as we know　正如我們所知
　　(D) be known for（ + 特點 ）「因～（ 特點 ）而聞名」，則用法不合。

5. (**A**) 依句意，大哥大是可以讓你「拿起來」，放在錢包或口袋裏的電話，故選 (A) ***pick up***「拿起來」。
　　(B) put up　舉起；張貼
　　(C) line up　排隊
　　(D) make up　化粧；編造；和好；組成

Pagers and cellular phones work *like regular phones*, <u>except</u> *they*
6
don't require telephone wires. They are based <u>on</u> a *relatively* new
7
technology *called wireless communications*.

呼叫器和大哥大,除了不需要電話線之外,功能就跟普通電話一樣。它們都是
根據一種相當新穎的科技設計而成,那就是「無線通訊」。

> work〔wɜk〕*v.* 運作　　regular〔'rɛgjələ〕*adj.* 平常的;普通的
> require〔rɪ'kwaɪr〕*v.* 需要　　wire〔waɪr〕*n.* 電線
> relatively〔'rɛlətɪvlɪ〕*adv.* 相當地
> wireless〔'waɪrlɪs〕*adj.* 無線的
> communications〔kə,mjunə'keʃənz〕*n. pl.* 通訊

6. (**B**)　呼叫器和大哥大「除了」不需要電話線外,其他功能都和普通的電話
　　　　一樣,故選 (B) *except*「除了~之外」。而 (A) 因為,(C) besides
　　　　「除了~之外,(還有…)」,與句意不合。而 (D) therefore「因
　　　　此」,也不合句意。

7. (**D**)　*be based on* 根據

Regardless of ***how** they work*, it is both a <u>status</u> symbol <u>and</u>
8　　　　　　　　　　　　　　　　　　　9　　　　　10
practical to carry a cell phone or a pager.

無論它們的功能如何,攜帶大哥大或呼叫器,不但是個地位象徵,而且也頗為
實用。

> practical〔'præktɪkl̩〕*adj.* 實用的

8. (**C**)　依句意,「無論」它們的功能如何,選 (C) *regardless of*「無論;
　　　　不管」。而 (A) whether「是否」,(B) despite「儘管」,(D) in
　　　　spite of「儘管」,均不合句意。

9.(**A**)　依句意，帶呼叫器和大哥大是「地位」的象徵，故選 (A) *status*
（ˈstetəs) *n.* 地位。
(B) statue（ˈstætʃu) *n.* 雕像
(C) stature（ˈstætʃɚ) *n.* 身材
(D) statute（ˈstætʃut) *n.* 法規

10.(**B**)　*both* A *and* B 表「A 和 B 兩者」，故選 (B)。

TEST 45

Read the following passage, and choose the best answer for each blank.

Frozen foods allow people to eat vegetables, fruits, and other ___1___ foods at any time of the year. It's a convenience that is easy to ___2___. But frozen foods ___3___ only since the early 1900's. An American inventor Mr. Birdseye gets the ___4___ for creating frozen food. He lived in northern Canada from 1914 to 1917. During that time, he studied the way ___5___ the Eskimos stored meat by freezing it outdoors. Months later, they would ___6___ the food and cook it. It almost ___7___ fresh. When Birdseye returned to the United States, he experimented with ___8___ food and selling it ___8___. People liked the idea and bought his food. Birdseye registered about 300 inventions, ___9___ his quick-freezing method, during his lifetime. Today, "Birdseye" is a popular ___10___ of frozen food.

1. A. daily
   B. weekly
   C. monthly
   D. seasonal

2. A. take for granted
   B. take into account
   C. take part in
   D. take a chance

3. A. exist
   B. existed
   C. have existed
   D. had existed

4. A. favor
   B. credit
   C. mission
   D. advantage

5. A. how
   B. by which
   C. with which
   D. in which

6. A. spoil
   B. thaw
   C. preserve
   D. dehydrate

7. A. tasted
   B. smelled
   C. looked
   D. felt

8. A. freezing; freezing
   B. frozen; frozen
   C. freezing; frozen
   D. frozen; freezing

9. A. include
   B. including
   C. included
   D. to include

10. A. brand
    B. trace
    C. sign
    D. signal

TEST 45 詳解

Frozen foods allow people to eat vegetables, fruits, and other

<u>seasonal</u> foods *at any time of the year.* It's a convenience *that is*
　　　1

easy to <u>take for granted</u>. ***But*** frozen foods <u>have existed</u> *only since*
　　　　　　　2　　　　　　　　　　　　　　　　　　　　3

the early 1900's.

　　冷凍食品可使人們在一年中的任何時候，吃到蔬菜、水果，以及其他季節性的食物。大家很容易會認爲這種便利是理所當然的。其實冷凍食品是從二十世紀初才開始存在的。

> frozen〔'frozn〕*adj.* 冷凍的
> ***frozen food*** 冷凍食品
> convenience〔kən'vinjəns〕*n.* 便利

1. (**D**) 依句意，冷凍食品讓人們能在一年的任何時候，吃到蔬菜、水果，以及其他「季節性的」食物，故選 (D) ***seasonal***〔'siznəl〕*adj.* 季節性的。
  (A) daily〔'delɪ〕*adj.* 每天的
  (B) weekly〔'wiklɪ〕*adj.* 每週的
  (C) monthly〔'mʌnθlɪ〕*adj.* 每月的

2. (**A**) 依句意，我們很容易會「認爲這種便利是理所當然的」，故選 (A) ***take sth. for granted*** 「視～爲理所當然」。
  (B) take *sth.* into account 考慮某事
  (C) take part in 參加
  (D) take a chance 冒險；碰運氣

3. (**C**) 依句意，冷凍食品是從二十世紀早期就存在了，故用「現在完成式」，
表示「從過去持續到現在的狀態」，故選 (C) *have existed*。
exist〔ɪgˈzɪst〕*v.* 存在

An American inventor, *Mr. Birdseye*, gets the credit *for creating*
<u>4</u>
frozen food. He lived *in northern Canada from 1914 to 1917.*
During that time, he studied the way *in which the Eskimos stored*
<u>5</u>
meat by freezing it outdoors. Months later, they would thaw the
<u>6</u>
food and cook it. It *almost* tasted fresh.
<u>7</u>

美國發明家伯宰先生，擁有發明冷凍食品的這項殊榮。他在一九一四至一九一
七年間，住在加拿大北部。在那段期間，他研究了愛斯基摩人保存肉類的方
法，那就是在戶外把肉冰凍起來。幾個月後，他們就能把食物解凍，並加以
烹煮。味道嚐起來就跟新鮮的差不多。

Eskimo〔ˈɛskəˌmo〕*n.* 愛斯基摩人　　store〔stor〕*v.* 儲存
freeze〔friz〕*v.* 結冰；冷凍　　outdoors〔ˈautˈdorz〕*adv.* 在戶外

4. (**B**) 依句意，美國發明家伯宰先生，擁有發明冷凍食品的這項「殊榮」，
故選 (B) *credit*〔ˈkrɛdɪt〕*n.* 榮譽。
(A) favor〔ˈfevɚ〕*n.* 恩惠
(C) mission〔ˈmɪʃən〕*n.* 任務
(D) advantage〔ədˈvæntɪdʒ〕*n.* 優點

5. (**D**) 愛斯基摩人是「以」此方法來保存肉類，介系詞 in 不可省略，故選 (D)
in which。which 代替先行詞 way。

6. (**B**) 依句意，幾個月後，愛斯基摩人就把食物「解凍」後才加以烹煮，故
選 (B) *thaw* 〔θɔ〕*v.* 解凍；退冰。
(A) spoil 〔spɔɪl〕*v.* 破壞
(C) preserve 〔prɪ'zɝv〕*v.* 保存
(D) dehydrate 〔di'haɪdret〕*v.* 使脫水

7. (**A**) 依句意，食物「嚐起來」和新鮮的差不多，故選 (A) *taste* 〔test〕*v.*
嚐起來。而 (B) smell 〔smɛl〕*v.* 聞起來，(C) look 〔lʊk〕*v.* 看起來，
(D) feel 〔fil〕*v.* 覺得，均不合句意。

When *Birdseye returned to the United States*, he experimented with
freezing food **and** selling it frozen. People liked the idea **and**
    8   8
bought his food. Birdseye registered about 300 inventions, *including*
                                         9
his quick-freezing method, *during his lifetime. Today,* "Birdseye" is a
popular brand *of frozen food.*
       10

當伯宰先生回到美國後，他將冷凍食物的方法加以實驗，並販售冷凍食品。大
家都喜愛這個發明，而購買他的產品。伯宰先生一生中，大約登記了三百種發
明，其中還包括了急速冷凍的方法。現在，「伯宰」已成為冷凍食品中相當受歡
迎的品牌。

experiment 〔ɪk'spɛrəmənt〕*v.* 實驗　　register〔'rɛdʒɪstɚ〕*v.* 登記
invention 〔ɪn'vɛnʃən〕*n.* 發明　　lifetime〔'laɪf,taɪm〕*n.* 一生

8. (**C**) 依句意，伯宰先生實驗「冷凍」食物的方法，需使用動詞 freeze，又
因前有介詞 with，故動詞 freeze 需改成動名詞 freezing。伯宰先生
還將食物以「冷凍的」形式出售，這裡 it 是指 food，其後加上受詞
補語來修飾 it，由於食物是「被冷凍的」，故用 frozen，選 (C)。

9. (**B**) 原句為 Birdseye registered about 300 inventions, which included his quick-freezing method, …，改為分詞構句後，省略 which，並將動詞改為現在分詞，故選 (B) including「包括」。

10. (**A**) 依句意，現在 Birdseye 已成為冷凍食品中最受歡迎的「品牌」，故選 (A) **brand**〔 brænd 〕*n.* 品牌。

  (B) trace〔 tres 〕*n.* 痕跡

  (C) sign〔 saɪn 〕*n.* 符號

  (D) signal〔ˈsɪgnḷ 〕*n.* 信號

TEST 46

Read the following passage, and choose the best answer for each blank.

    The heart of the celebration of Christmas ___1___ gifts. ___2___ the approach of Christmas, children all over the world look forward to the coming of a mysterious man, who will ___3___ gifts ___3___ good children. Of course, gifts are handled by different men in different countries. In America, it is Santa Claus that brings gifts. He travels on a sleigh ___4___ by flying reindeer. In Spain, the three Magi come on January 6 and ___5___ children's shoes ___5___ goodies. In other European countries, ___6___ is taken care of by Saint Nicholas of Myra. He comes on December 5 or ___7___ Christmas Eve, and brings a group of ___8___ assistants. In the Netherlands, Black Peter helps Saint Nicholas. Parents also like the idea of Christmas gifts because children ___9___ behave themselves, ___10___ to get presents at Christmas.

1. A. lies in
   B. thanks to
   C. comes about
   D. results from

2. A. At
   B. With
   C. To
   D. During

3. A. bring; about
   B. leave; for
   C. buy; to
   D. play; with

4. A. driven
   B. ridden
   C. drawn
   D. pushed

5. A. fill; with
   B. full; of
   C. are filled; with
   D. are full; of

6. A. giving-gift
   B. gift-giving
   C. gifts-giving
   D. gift-given

7. A. in
   B. at
   C. on
   D. by

8. A. weird-dressed
   B. dressed-weirdly
   C. weirdly-dressed
   D. dressing-weird

9. A. likely to
   B. tend to
   C. apt to
   D. liable to

10. A. hope
    B. to hope
    C. and hoping
    D. hoping

TEST 46 詳解

The heart *of the celebration of Christmas* lies in gifts. *With the*

1   2

approach of Christmas, children *all over the world* look forward to

the coming *of a mysterious man*, *who* will *leave* gifts *for* good

                             3   3

children.

聖誕節的慶祝活動，重點就在禮物。隨著聖誕節的來臨，全世界的小孩，
都在期待一位神祕人物的到來，他會給乖小孩留下禮物。

> heart〔hɑrt〕*n.* 重點；重心
> approach〔ə'protʃ〕*n.* 接近
> **look forward to** 期待
> mysterious〔mɪs'tɪrɪəs〕*adj.* 神祕的

1. (**A**) 依句意，重點就「在」禮物，故選 (A) *lie in*「在於」。而 (B)
   thanks to「由於」(= *owing to* = *because of*)，(C) come
   about「發生」(= *happen*)，(D) result from「起因於」，均不合。

2. (**B**) 表示「隨著」，介系詞用 with，選 (B)。
   with the approach of ~ 隨著~的接近

3. (**B**) 依句意，選 (B) *leave sth. for sb.*「留給某人某物」。而 (A) 應改為
   bring *sth.* for *sb.*「帶某物給某人」，(C) 應改為 buy *sth.* for *sb.*
   「買某物給某人」，(D) play *sth.* with *sb.*「和某人玩某物」，與
   句意不合。

Of course, gifts are handled *by different men in different countries.*

In America, it is Santa Claus *that brings gifts.* He travels *on a*

sleigh drawn by flying reindeer. In Spain, the three Magi come
____4

on January 6 and fill children's shoes *with goodies.*
⎯⎯⎯⎯⎯⎯⎯⎯⎯5⎯⎯⎯⎯⎯⎯⎯⎯⎯⎯⎯⎯⎯5

當然，不同的國家，掌管送禮的人就不同。在美國，送禮物的人是聖誕老人，
他會駕著一輛，由會飛的麋鹿所拉著的雪橇，遊走四方。在西班牙，三位朝聖
者會在每年一月六日降臨，並在孩子們的鞋子裡裝滿好吃的東西。

      handle〔'hændl〕*v.* 處理

      Santa Claus〔'sæntə,klɔz〕*n.* 聖誕老人

      sleigh〔sle〕*n.* 雪橇   reindeer〔'rendɪr〕*n.* 麋鹿

      Magi〔'medʒaɪ〕*n.* 朝聖者

      the three Magi 聖經內自東方趕來對初生聖嬰禮拜的三位朝聖者

      goody〔'gʊdɪ〕*n.* 好吃的東西；糖果

4. (**C**) 依句意，聖誕老人會駕著一輛會飛的麋鹿所「拉」著的雪橇，故選 (C)
      drawn。   draw〔drɔ〕*v.* 拖；拉

      (A) drive〔draɪv〕*v.* 駕駛；驅趕

      (B) ride〔raɪd〕*v.* 騎乘

      (D) push〔pʊʃ〕*v.* 推

5. (**A**) 依句意，三位朝聖者會在鞋子裡「裝滿」好吃的東西，故選 (A)。
      fill A *with* B 用 B 裝滿 A

      (C) be filled with「充滿了～」= (D) be full of，均表狀態，在此
      不合。

In other European countries, <u>gift-giving</u> is taken care of by Saint
6

Nicholas of Myra. He comes on December 5 or <u>on</u> Christmas Eve,
7

and brings a group of <u>weirdly-dressed</u> assistants. In the Netherlands,
8

Black Peter helps Saint Nicholas.

在其他歐洲國家，送禮物的任務是由麥拉的聖尼古拉斯負責。他會在十二月
五日，或聖誕夜來，並且帶著一群穿著怪異的助手。在荷蘭，則是由黑彼德
來協助聖尼古拉斯分送禮物。

> *take care of* 處理
> *Saint Nicholas* 聖尼古拉斯；聖誕老人（即 *Santa Claus*）
> Myra (ˈmaɪrə) *n.* 麥拉（小亞細亞西南部 Lycia 之一古都）
> assistant (əˈsɪstənt) *n.* 助手　　Netherlands (ˈnɛðələndz) *n.* 荷蘭

6. (**B**)　依句意，選(B) *gift-giving*「送禮物」。

7. (**C**)　表示特定日子的早、午、晚，介系詞用 on，選 (C)。

8. (**C**)　依句意，選 (C) *weirdly-dressed*「穿著怪異的」。
　　　　weirdly (ˈwɪrdlɪ) *adv.* 怪異地

Parents *also* like the idea of Christmas gifts *because* children <u>tend</u>
9

<u>to</u> behave themselves, <u>hoping</u> to get presents at Christmas.
10

做父母的也很喜歡聖誕禮物，因為小孩子希望能在聖誕節得到禮物，所以就會
守規矩。

> *behave oneself* 守規矩　　present (ˈprɛznt) *n.* 禮物

9. (**B**)　小孩「比較會」守規矩，故選 (B) ***tend to***「易於；傾向於」。
　　而 (A) (C) (D)均為形容詞片語，必須有 be 動詞，(A) be likely to
　　「可能」，(C) be apt to「易於」，(D) be liable to「易於」，
　　用法均不合。

10. (**D**)　原句為…because children who hope to get presents at
　　Christmas tend to behave themselves. 將形容詞子句 who…at
　　Christmas 改為分詞構句，須去掉關係代名詞 who，並將動詞改為
　　現在分詞 hoping，故選 (D)。

TEST 47

Read the following passage, and choose the best answer for each blank.

Many offices today have computers. Computers ___1___
to calculate numbers and ___2___ information quickly and
easily around the world. But some bosses are discovering
that office workers use their computers to play computer
games! Too much game-playing not only ___3___ time but
might ___4___ the system. A few companies have ___5___
game-playing at work. But this doesn't always ___6___ .
Many games have special features that ___7___ them. With
a push of one button, called a "panic" button, a game on the
computer screen ___8___ and can be quickly changed into
columns of numbers. If game players want to avoid panic
and ___9___ by the boss, this special ___10___ is a great help.

1. A. make that possible
   B. make this possibly
   C. make it possible
   D. make it possibly

2. A. translate
   B. transport
   C. transfer
   D. transfuse

3. A. saves
   B. wastes
   C. tells
   D. keeps

4. A. overflow
   B. overlook
   C. overload
   D. overthrow

5. A. forbidden
   B. allowed
   C. permitted
   D. offered

6. A. effect
   B. influence
   C. work
   D. affect

7. A. pretend
   B. protect
   C. delete
   D. disguise

8. A. appears
   B. vanishes
   C. exposes
   D. uncovers

9. A. getting caught
   B. to be caught
   C. caught
   D. get caught

10. A. demand
    B. recommend
    C. remind
    D. command

TEST 47 詳解

Many offices *today* have computers. Computers <u>make it</u>
1

<u>possible</u> to calculate numbers *and* <u>transfer</u> information *quickly and*
2

easily around the world.

現在很多辦公室都有電腦。電腦可以計算數字，還可以旣快速又容易地將
資訊傳送至全世界。

calculate〔'kælkjə,let〕*v.* 計算　　***around the world*** 全世界

1. (**C**) ***make it possible to* V.**「使～成爲可能」；it 爲虛受詞，代替眞正
的受詞 to calculate numbers…the world.

2. (**C**) 電腦可以將資訊「傳送」至全世界，故選 (C) ***transfer***〔træns'fʒ〕
v. 轉移；傳送。而 (A) translate〔træns'let〕*v.* 翻譯，(B) transport
〔træns'port〕*v.* 運送，(D) transfuse〔træns'fjuz〕*v.* 輸（血），均
不合句意。

But some bosses are discovering *that* office workers use their

computers *to play computer games*! Too much game-playing *not*

only <u>wastes</u> time *but* might <u>overload</u> the system. A few
3　　　　　　　　　　　　4

companies have <u>forbidden</u> game-playing *at work.* *But* this doesn't
5

always <u>work</u>.
6

不過有些老闆卻發現，公司員工會利用電腦玩電腦遊戲！遊戲玩太多，不只會
浪費時間，而且可能使系統超載。有些公司已禁止在工作時玩電腦遊戲。不過
這項規定不一定有效。

> boss〔bɔs〕*n.* 老板　　discover〔dɪˋskʌvɚ〕*v.* 發現
> ***not only***…***but*** (***also***)～　不僅…而且～
> ***at work***　工作時

3. (**B**) 玩太多電腦遊戲會「浪費」時間，故選 (B) ***waste***〔west〕*v.* 浪費。
    (A) save〔sev〕*v.* 節省
    (C) tell time　報時；懂得看時間
    (D) keep good / bad time　（鐘錶）走得準/不準

4. (**C**) 依句意，玩太多電腦遊戲會使系統「超載」，故選 (C) ***overload***
    〔ˋovɚ͵lod〕*v.* 超載。
    (A) overflow〔ˋovɚ͵flo〕*v.* 溢出；氾濫
    (B) overlook〔ˋovɚ͵lʊk〕*v.* 忽視
    (D) overthrow〔ˋovɚ͵θro〕*v.* 推翻

5. (**A**) 依句意，公司「禁止」員工在工作時玩電腦遊戲，故選(A) ***forbid***
    〔fɚˋbɪd〕*v.* 禁止。
    (B) allow〔əˋlaʊ〕*v.* 允許
    (C) permit〔pɚˋmɪt〕*v.* 允許
    (D) offer〔ˋɔfɚ〕*v.* 提供

6. (**C**) 依句意，這項規定並不一定「有效」，故選 (C) ***work***「（計畫、方法
    等）有效」。
    (A) effect〔ɪˋfɛkt〕*n.* 效果；影響
    (B) influence〔ˋɪnflʊəns〕*n. v.* 影響
    (D) affect〔əˋfɛkt〕*v.* 影響

Many games have special features *that disguise them.* *With a push*
<u> 7</u>

of one button, called a "panic" button, a game *on the computer*

screen <u>vanishes</u> *and* can be *quickly* changed into columns of
<u> 8</u>

numbers.

許多遊戲有特殊功能來掩飾自己。只要按一個叫做「恐慌」的鈕，電腦螢幕上
的遊戲畫面就會消失，而且會很快地轉變成好幾欄的數字。

> feature〔'fitʃɚ〕*n.* 特點 　　 push〔pʊʃ〕*n.* 按
> button〔'bʌtṇ〕*n.* 按鈕 　　 panic〔'pænɪk〕*n.* 恐慌
> screen〔skrin〕*n.* 螢幕 　　 *be changed into* 變成
> column〔'kɑləm〕*n.* 欄

7. (**D**) 依句意，許多電腦遊戲有特殊功能來「掩飾」自己，故選 (D)
　　　　 disguise〔dɪs'gaɪz〕*v.* 偽裝；掩飾。
　　　　 (A) pretend〔prɪ'tɛnd〕*v.* 假裝（為不及物動詞，在此用法不合）
　　　　 (B) protect〔prə'tɛkt〕*v.* 保護
　　　　 (C) delete〔dɪ'lit〕*v.* 刪除

8. (**B**) 依句意，只要按一個叫做「恐慌」的鈕，電腦螢幕上的遊戲畫面就
　　　　 會「消失」，故選 (B) *vanish*〔'vænɪʃ〕*v.* 消失。
　　　　 (A) appear〔ə'pɪr〕*v.* 出現
　　　　 (C) expose〔ɪk'spoz〕*v.* 暴露
　　　　 (D) uncover〔ʌn'kʌvɚ〕*v.* 揭開；洩露

*If game players want to avoid panic **and** getting caught by the*
                                                9

boss, this special <u>command</u> is a great help.
                     10

如果玩遊戲的人想要避免驚慌失措，或不想被老闆逮到，這個特殊指令會有莫大的幫助。

9. (**A**)　*avoid* + *N*./ *Ving*「避免～」，且依句意，玩遊戲的人不想「被逮到」，須用被動語態，故選 (A) *getting caught*。

10. (**D**)　這個「指令」會有莫大的幫助，故選 (D) *command* 〔 kəˈmænd 〕 *n.* 命令；指令。

    (A) demand 〔 dɪˈmænd 〕 *n.* 要求

    (B) recommend 〔 ˌrɛkəˈmɛnd 〕 *v.* 推薦

    (C) remind 〔 rɪˈmaɪnd 〕 *v.* 提醒；使想起

TEST 48

Read the following passage, and choose the best answer for each blank.

"Ferris wheel" is the name of a popular amusement park ride. Children sitting in baskets are ___1___ high up into the sky by an enormous, vertical revolving wheel. The Ferris wheel, named ___2___ its American inventor George Ferris Jr., ___3___ 100 years old in 1993. The very first Ferris wheel was seen — and ridden — by people ___4___ the World's Columbian Exposition in Chicago. It was 250 feet ___5___ diameter and had a height of 264 feet. That is six times ___6___ than most Ferris wheels built today. It ___7___ 20 minutes for that wheel to turn around once. Thrillseekers paid 50 cents to ___8___ a turn. Today, Ferris wheels are still the ___9___ of any amusement park, carnival or state fair. Children and adults love the view from the top and the ___10___ sensation of dropping back to earth.

1. A. risen
   B. lifted
   C. elevating
   D. promoting

2. A. of
   B. as
   C. to
   D. after

3. A. made
   B. took
   C. turned
   D. kept

4. A. visit
   B. visited
   C. visiting
   D. to visit

5. A. in
   B. by
   C. of
   D. with

6. A. older
   B. longer
   C. higher
   D. smaller

7. A. spent
   B. cost
   C. passed
   D. took

8. A. take
   B. ride
   C. make
   D. do

9. A. mainstream
   B. centerpiece
   C. masterpiece
   D. spotlight

10. A. afraid
    B. scary
    C. fearless
    D. frightened

TEST 48 詳解

"Ferris wheel" is the name *of a popular amusement park ride.*

Children *sitting in baskets* are lifted *high up into the sky by an*
                                        1

enormous, vertical revolving wheel.

　　「摩天輪」是遊樂園裡，一種很受歡迎的遊樂設施之名稱。摩天輪是個巨
大的、垂直旋轉的輪子，會將坐在籃子裡的小孩，高舉至空中。

> wheel〔hwil〕*n.* 輪子
> Ferris wheel〔'fɛrɪs͵hwil〕*n.* 摩天輪
> amusement〔ə'mjuzmənt〕*n.* 娛樂
> ***amusement park*** 遊樂園
> ride〔raɪd〕*n.*（供乘坐的）遊樂設施
> basket〔'bæskɪt〕*n.* 籃子
> enormous〔ɪ'nɔrməs〕*adj.* 巨大的
> vertical〔'vɝtɪkḷ〕*adj.* 垂直的
> revolving〔rɪ'vɑlvɪŋ〕*adj.* 旋轉的

1.(**B**) 坐在籃子裏的小孩，「被高舉」至空中，依句意爲被動語態，故選
　　　　(B) ***lifted***。　lift〔lɪft〕*v.* 舉起
　　　　(A) rise〔raɪz〕*v.* 上升（無被動語態）
　　　　(C) elevate〔'ɛlə͵vet〕*v.* 舉起（須改爲 elevated 才能選）
　　　　(D) promote〔prə'mot〕*v.* 提倡；升遷

The Ferris wheel, *named after its American inventor George Ferris*
　　　　　　　　　　　　　2

Jr., turned 100 years old *in 1993*. The very first Ferris wheel
　　　3

was seen — and ridden — *by people visiting the World's Columbian*
　　　　　　　　　　　　　　　　　　　4

Exposition in Chicago.

摩天輪這個名稱，是以它的美國籍發明人小喬治‧菲利斯，而命名的。摩天輪到
一九九三年就一百歲了。最先見到並乘坐有史以來第一個摩天輪的人，就是當
時參加芝加哥世界哥倫布博覽會的人。

　　Jr. = Junior 小
　　Columbian〔kə'lʌmbɪən〕*adj.* 美洲的；哥倫布的
　　exposition〔͵ɛkspə'zɪʃən〕*n.* 博覽會

2. (**D**) *be named after* 以～的名字命名
　　　原句是由 which was named after…簡化而來。

3. (**C**) 依句意，摩天輪「就」一百歲了，故選 (C) *turned*「超過（某年齡）；
　　　已到達」。

4. (**C**) 原句為…by people who visited the world's…，將 who 所引導
　　　的形容詞子句改為分詞構句，須省略關係代名詞 who，並將動詞改
　　　為現在分詞 visiting，故選 (C)。

It was 250 feet *in diameter **and*** had a height *of 264 feet.* That is
　　　　　　　　5

six times <u>higher</u> *than most Ferris wheels built today.* It <u>took</u> 20
　　　　　　6　　　　　　　　　　　　　　　　　　　　　　　7

minutes *for that wheel to turn around once.* Thrillseekers paid 50

cents *to <u>take</u> a turn.*
　　　8

最早的摩天輪,其直徑有二百五十英呎,高二百六十四英呎,是現在大多數摩天輪的六倍高,轉一次需要二十分鐘。追求刺激的人來坐一次,需要花五十分錢。

　　　　diameter〔daɪˋæmətə〕*n.* 直徑
　　　　height〔haɪt〕*n.* 高度
　　　　thrillseeker〔ˋθrɪlˏsikə〕*n.* 追求刺激的人

5.(**A**) 表「在～方面;在～部位」,介詞用 in,故選 (A)。

6.(**C**) 依句意,第一個摩天輪的是現在摩天輪的六倍「高」,故選 (C) *higher*。

7.(**D**) It + takes + *sb.* + 時間、勞力 + to V. 花費某人～(時間 / 勞力)

8.(**A**) *take a turn*(駕車、騎馬、玩遊樂設施)兜一圈;玩一次

Today, Ferris wheels are *still* the centerpiece *of any amusement*
　　　　　　　　　　　　　　　　　　　9
park, carnival or state fair. Children and adults love the view

*from the top **and** the* scary sensation *of dropping back to earth*.
　　　　　　　　　　　　10
現在,摩天輪仍然是任何遊樂園、嘉年華會,以及各州的博覽會上的焦點。大人和小孩,都很喜歡從最高點所看到的景色,以及那種要掉到地上的可怕感覺。

　　　　carnival〔ˋkɑrnəvḷ〕*n.* 嘉年華會
　　　　state〔stet〕*adj.* 州的
　　　　fair〔fɛr〕*n.* 博覽會
　　　　view〔vju〕*n.* 景色
　　　　sensation〔sɛnˋseʃən〕*n.* 感覺

9. (**B**) 依句意，摩天輪是許多場合的「焦點；重點」，故選 (B) *centerpiece*
〔'sɛntɚ͵pis 〕 *n.* 焦點。

(A) mainstream 〔'men͵strim 〕 *n.* (傾向、潮流之) 主流

(C) masterpiece 〔'mæstɚ͵pis 〕 *n.* 傑作；名著

(D) spotlight 〔'spɑt͵laɪt 〕 *n.* 聚光燈

10. (**B**) 依句意，要掉到地上的那種「可怕的」感覺，選 (B) *scary* 〔'skærɪ 〕
adj. 可怕的。而 (A) afraid 〔 ə'fred 〕 *adj.* (人) 害怕的，(C) fearless
〔'fɪrlɪs 〕 *adj.* (人) 勇敢的，(D) frightened 〔'fraɪtṇd 〕 *adj.* (人) 害怕
的，用法與句意皆不合。

TEST 49

Read the following passage, and choose the best answer for each blank.

Are you aware of the striking similarities ___1___ two of the most popular U.S. presidents, Abraham Lincoln and John F. Kennedy? A minor point is that the names Lincoln and Kennedy both have seven letters. Both men had their elections legally ___2___. Lincoln and Kennedy are both remembered ___3___ their sense of humor as well as ___4___ their interest in civil rights. Lincoln became president in 1860; Kennedy, in 1960. Lincoln's secretary was Mrs. Kennedy; Kennedy's secretary was Mrs. Lincoln. Neither man took the advice of his secretary not to make a ___5___ appearance on the day ___6___ he was assassinated. Lincoln and Kennedy were both killed on a Friday ___7___ the presence of their wives. Both assassins, John Wilkes Booth and Lee Harvey Oswald, have fifteen letters in their names, and both were murdered before they could be ___8___ to trial. Just as Lincoln was succeeded by a Southern Democrat named Johnson, ___9___ was Kennedy. Andrew Johnson (Lincoln's successor) was born in 1808; Lyndon Johnson (Kennedy's successor) was born in 1908. And ___10___ , the same two-wheeled ammunition car carried the bodies of both men in their funeral processions.

1. A. among
   B. between
   C. with
   D. in

2. A. challenge
   B. challenged
   C. challenging
   D. challenges

3. A. for
   B. in
   C. to
   D. about

4. A. for
   B. in
   C. to
   D. about

5. A. private
   B. public
   C. open
   D. official

6. A. which
   B. that
   C. on which
   D. in that

7. A. in
   B. to
   C. with
   D. before

8. A. carried
   B. brought
   C. taken
   D. fetched

9. A. also
   B. so
   C. as
   D. same

10. A. firstly
    B. finally
    C. consequently
    D. therefore

TEST 49 詳解

Are you aware of the striking similarities *between two of the*
$\underset{1}{}$
most popular U.S. presidents, Abraham Lincoln and John F.

Kennedy?

你有沒有察覺到，美國兩位最受歡迎的總統，亞伯拉罕・林肯以及約翰・
甘迺迪之間，有驚人的雷同之處？

> **be aware of** 察覺到   striking ('straıkıŋ) *adj.* 明顯的；驚人的
> similarity (,sımə'lærətı) *n.* 相似

1. (**B**) 依句意，兩位總統「之間」的雷同處，故選 (B) **between**。
   而 (A) among 則用於「三者之間」，在此不合。

A minor point is *that the names Lincoln and Kennedy both have*

seven letters. Both men had their elections *legally* challenged.
$\underset{2}{}$

Lincoln and Kennedy are both remembered *for their sense of*
$\underset{3}{}$

humor as well as for their interest in civil rights.
$\underset{4}{}$

比較次要的一點，就是他們的名字，Lincoln 和 Kennedy，都有七個字母。兩
人選舉時，其合法性都受人質疑。林肯和甘迺迪兩人的幽默感，以及他們對人
權的關注，仍為人們所懷念。

> minor ('maınə) *adj.* 較小的；較次要的   letter ('lɛtə) *n.* 字母
> legally ('ligḷı) *adv.* 法律上；合法地   **a sense of humor** 幽默感
> civil ('sıvḷ) *adj.* 公民的   **civil rights** 民權

2. (**B**)「使役動詞 have / make + O. + 過去分詞」表被動，故選 (B)。
　　challenge (ˈtʃælɪndʒ) *v.* 質疑；挑戰

3. (**A**) 依句意，林肯和甘迺迪是「因為」幽默感及對人權的關注，而為人們
　　所懷念，故選 (A) *for*「因為」。

4. (**A**) *as well as*「以及」，為一對等連接詞，須連接兩個文法作用相同的
　　單字、片語或子句，故選 (A) *for*。

Lincoln became president *in 1860*; Kennedy, *in 1960*. Lincoln's

secretary was Mrs. Kennedy; Kennedy's secretary was Mrs.

Lincoln. Neither man took the advice *of his secretary* not to make

a <u>public</u> appearance [*on the day* *on **which*** he was assassinated.
　　 5 　　　　　　　　　　　　　　　　6

林肯在一八六〇年當選總統，而甘迺迪是在一九六〇年。林肯的祕書是姓甘迺
迪的女士，而甘迺迪的秘書姓林肯。兩人在被暗殺的那一天，都沒有聽從他們
秘書的勸告，不要公開露面。

　　　　advice (ədˈvaɪs) *n.* 勸告　　appearance (əˈpɪrəns) *n.* 出現
　　　　assassinate (əˈsæsn̩͵et) *v.* 暗殺

5. (**B**) 依句意，祕書都建議他們不要做「公開的」露面，故選 (B) *public*「公
　　開的」。而 (A) private (ˈpraɪvɪt) *adj.* 私人的，(C) 開放的，(D) official
　　(əˈfɪʃəl) *adj.* 官方的，均不合。

6. (**C**) 關係代名詞作介詞的受詞時，介詞可置於 whom 和 which 的前面或後
　　面，但絕不可省略，依句意，在兩位總統被暗殺的那一天，為一特定
　　日子，故介系詞用 on，選 (C)。

Lincoln and Kennedy were both killed *on a Friday in the presence*
7
of their wives. Both assassins, *John Wilkes Booth and Lee Harvey*
Oswald, have fifteen letters *in their names, **and*** both were
murdered ***before*** *they could be* <u>*brought*</u> *to trial.*
8

林肯和甘迺迪都是在星期五,而且是在他們的妻子面前被暗殺。兩名殺手,
John Wilkes Booth 和 Lee Harvey Oswald,名字都有十五個字母,而且
他們兩個人,都在送審前就被謀殺。

> assassin (ə'sæsın) *n.* 殺手;刺客　　murder ('mɝdə) *v.* 謀殺
> trial ('traɪəl) *n.* 審判

7. (**A**) *in the presence of* ~ 在~的面前　presence ('prɛzns) *n.* 面前

8. (**B**) *bring sb.* *to trial* 讓某人接受審判

Just ***as*** *Lincoln was succeeded by a Southern Democrat named*
Johnson, <u>*so*</u> *was Kennedy.* Andrew Johnson (*Lincoln's successor*)
9
was born *in 1808;* Lyndon Johnson (*Kennedy's successor*) was
born *in 1908.* ***And*** <u>*finally*</u>, the same two-wheeled ammunition
10
car carried the bodies *of both men in their funeral processions.*

接任林肯的人,是一名來自美國南方,名叫詹森的民主黨員,而接任甘迺迪的人也是。安德魯·詹森(林肯的繼任者),出生於一八○八年,而林登·詹森(甘迺迪的繼任者),則出生於一九○八年。最後一點是,在送葬的行列中,用來裝運兩位總統遺體的兩輪彈藥車,竟然是同一部。

succeed〔 sək'sid 〕v. 繼任;接任
Democrat〔'dɛmə,kræt 〕n. 美國民主黨員
successor〔 sək'sɛsɚ 〕n. 繼任者
ammunition〔,æmjə'nıʃən 〕n. 軍火;彈藥　　carry〔'kærı 〕v. 裝載
body〔'bɑdı 〕n. 屍體　　funeral〔'fjunərəl 〕n. 葬禮
procession〔 prə'sɛʃən 〕n. 行列

9. (**B**)　so 置於句首時,主詞與動詞須倒裝,即「so + 動詞 + 主詞」,表「~也是如此」。

10. (**B**)　依句意,選 (B) *finally*「最後」。而 (A) firstly「首先」, (C) consequently「因此」, (D) therefore「因此」,皆不合句意。

TEST 50

Read the following passage, and choose the best answer for each blank.

When we think of a detective, we think first of Sherlock Holmes. Even now, 100 years after the first story about him, he is still __1__ detective of all. __2__ still go to Baker Street, in London, to see the place __3__ he had his flat. There are films about him, pictures of him — we all know what he __4__, and what kind of clothes he __5__.

And yet Sherlock Holmes never __6__. The stories about him are just stories. So why do we remember him?

It is because he loves catching criminals. Sherlock Holmes chases criminals __7__ a hunter chases a fox. He is a bloodhound, a police dog, with his nose to the ground — __8__ criminals to the end of the world. Criminals may try __9__ — but when Sherlock Holmes has started the chase, we know that he will finish it __10__ a "kill."

1. A. a great
   B. the greatest
   C. a greatest
   D. greatest

2. A. Tourists
   B. Customers
   C. Inhabitants
   D. Curios

3. A. which
   B. on which
   C. where
   D. that

4. A. looked like
   B. looked alike
   C. looked
   D. seemed

5. A. had worn
   B. has worn
   C. wears
   D. wore

6. A. persisted
   B. resisted
   C. insisted
   D. existed

7. A. as
   B. when
   C. if
   D. though

8. A. follows
   B. followed
   C. following
   D. follow

9. A. hiding
   B. to hide
   C. hidden
   D. hide

10. A. with
    B. by
    C. in
    D. without

TEST 50 詳解

When we *think* of a *detective*, we *think* first of Sherlock Holmes. *Even now*, *100 years after the first story about him*, he is *still* the greatest detective *of all*. Tourists *still* go to Baker Street, *in London*, to see the place *where he had his flat*. There are films *about him*, pictures *of him* — we all know *what he looked like*, *and what* kind of clothes he wore.

一想到偵探，我們第一個就會想到福爾摩斯。即使在現在，雖然第一個關於他的故事至今已一百年了，他仍是所有偵探中最偉大的。仍有觀光客會到倫敦的貝克街，去看他公寓的所在地。有很多關於他的電影以及照片，所以我們都知道他長什麼樣子，穿哪一種衣服。

> detective〔dɪˋtɛktɪv〕n. 偵探
> Sherlock Holmes〔ˋʃɝlɑkˋhomz〕n. 夏洛克・福爾摩斯
> flat〔flæt〕n. 公寓　　film〔fɪlm〕n. 電影

1. (**B**) 在所有的偵探中，他是「最偉大的」，依句意用最高級，故選 (B) **the greatest**。

2. (**A**) 「觀光客」會去倫敦參觀他的房子，故選 (A) **tourist**〔ˋturɪst〕n. 觀光客。而 (B) customer〔ˋkʌstəmɚ〕n. 顧客，(C) inhabitant〔ɪnˋhæbətənt〕n. 居民，(D) curio〔ˋkjurɪ‚o〕n. 古董，均不合句意。

3. (**C**) 原句為 the place in which he had his flat. 而 in which 相當於 where，故選 (C)。

4. (**A**) 依句意，我們都知道「他長什麼樣子」，故選 (A) **what he looked like**。

5. (**D**) 依句意為過去式，故選 (D) **wore**。　wear〔wɛr〕v. 穿

And yet Sherlock Holmes *never* existed. The stories *about him*
                                        6
are just stories. ***So*** why do we remember him?

It is ***because*** *he loves catching criminals*. Sherlock Holmes

chases criminals *as a hunter chases a fox*. He is a bloodhound,
                  7
a police dog, with his nose to the ground—*following criminals*
                                                      8
to the end of the world. Criminals may try *to hide*—***but when***
                                                      9
Sherlock Holmes has started the chase, we know ***that*** he will

finish it *with* a "kill."
          10

　　然而，福爾摩斯是不存在的。有關他的故事也只是故事而已。那我們為什
麼還要懷念他呢？
　　原因就是他熱衷於逮捕罪犯。福爾摩斯追捕犯人，就好像獵人追捕狐狸一
樣，他就像是警犬，一種大型的偵察獵犬，把鼻子貼在地上——追著犯人到天
涯海角。犯人可能會企圖躲藏，不過一旦福爾摩斯展開他的追捕行動，我們都
清楚最後的結果，將會是「格殺勿論」。

criminal〔'krımənḷ〕*n.* 罪犯　　chase〔tʃes〕*n.* 追捕
bloodhound〔'blʌd,haund〕*n.* 大型的偵察獵犬　　***police dog*** 警犬

6. (**D**)　依句意，福爾摩斯是不「存在」的，故選 (D) ***exist***〔ɪg'zɪst〕*v.* 存在。
　　　而 (A) persist〔pɚ'sɪst〕*v.* 堅持，(B) resist〔rɪ'zɪst〕*v.* 抵抗，
　　　(C) insist〔ɪn'sɪst〕*v.* 堅持，均不合句意。

7. (**A**)　依句意，選 (A) ***as***「就像～」。

8. (**C**)　兩動詞當中無連接詞，第二個動詞要改成現在分詞，故選 (C)
　　　following。

9. (**B**)　依句意，犯人可能「企圖」躲藏，故選 (B)。「try＋to V.」，表「企
　　　圖～」，而「try＋V-ing」，則表「試驗」。

10. (**A**)　此處表「以」格殺勿論作為結束，故介系詞用 ***with***，選 (A)。

附錄

全民英語能力分級檢定測驗簡介

　　「全民英語能力分級檢定測驗」(General English Proficiency Test)，簡稱「全民英檢」(GEPT)，旨在提供我國各階段英語學習者一套公平、有效且可靠之英語能力評量工具，測驗對象包括在校學生及一般社會人士，可做為學習成果檢定、教學改進及公民營機構甄選人才等之參考。

　　本測驗為標準參照測驗 (criterion-referenced test)，參考我國英語教育體制，制定分級標準，整套系統共分五級──初級 (Elementary)、中級 (Intermediate)、中高級 (High-Intermediate)、高級 (Advanced)、優級 (Superior)。每級訂有明確能力標準，報考者可依英語能力選擇適當級數報考，每級均包含聽、說、讀、寫四項完整的測驗，通過所報考級數的能力標準即可取得該級的合格證書。

中級英語能力測驗簡介

I. 通過中級檢定者的英語能力

聽	讀	寫	說
在日常生活情境中，能聽懂一般的會話；能大致聽懂公共場所廣播、氣象報告及廣告等。在工作情境中，能聽懂簡易的產品介紹與操作說明。能大致聽懂外籍人士的談話及詢問。	在日常生活情境中，能閱讀短文、故事、私人信件、廣告、傳單、簡介及使用說明等。在工作情境中，能閱讀工作須知、公告、操作手冊、例行的文件、傳真、電報等。	能寫簡單的書信、故事及心得等。對於熟悉且與個人經歷相關的主題，能以簡易的文字表達。	在日常生活情境中，能以簡易英語交談或描述一般事物，能介紹自己的生活作息、工作、家庭、經歷等，並可對一般話題陳述看法。在工作情境中，能進行簡單的答詢，並與外籍人士交談溝通。

II. 測驗項目

	初　試		複　試	
測驗項目	聽力測驗	閱讀能力測驗	寫作能力測驗	口說能力測驗
總題數	45 題	40 題	2 題	13~14 題
作答時間	約 30 分鐘	45 分鐘	40 分鐘	約 15 分鐘
測驗內容	看圖辨義 問答 簡短對話	詞彙和結構 段落填空 閱讀理解	中譯英 英文作文	朗讀短文 回答問題 看圖敘述
總測驗時間 （含試前、 試後說明）	兩項一共約需 2 小時		約需 1 小時	約需 1 小時

　　聽力及閱讀能力測驗成績採標準計分方式，滿分 120 分。寫作及口說能力測驗成績採整體式評分，使用級分制，分為 0~5 級分，再轉換成百分制。各項成績通過標準如下：

III. 成績計算及通過標準

初試	通過標準	滿分	複試	通過標準	滿分
聽力測驗 閱讀能力測驗	兩項測驗成績總和達 160 分，且其中任一項成績不低於 72 分。（自 97 年起生效，不溯及既往）	120 120	寫作能力測驗 口說能力測驗	80 80	100 100

IV. 寫作能力測驗級分說明

第一部份：中譯英

級分	分數	説　　　　　　　　　　明
5	40	內容能充分表達題意，文段 (text) 結構及連貫性甚佳。用字遣詞、文法、拼字、標點及大小寫幾乎無誤。
4	32	內容適切表達題意，句子結構及連貫性大致良好。用字遣詞、文法、拼字、標點及大小寫偶有錯誤，但不妨礙題意之表達。
3	34	內容未能完全表達題意，句子結構鬆散，連貫性不足。用字遣詞及文法有誤，但不妨礙題意之表達，且拼字、標點及大小寫也有錯誤。
2	16	僅能局部表達原文題意，句子結構不良、有誤，且大多難以理解並缺乏連貫性。字彙有限，文法、拼字、標點及大小寫有許多錯誤。
1	8	內容無法表達題意，語句沒有結構概念及連貫性，無法理解。字彙極有限，文法、拼字、標點及大小寫之錯誤多且嚴重。
0	0	未答/等同未答。

第二部份：英文作文

級分	分數	説　　　　　　　　　　明
5	60	內容適切表達題目要求，組織甚佳，靈活運用字彙及句型，句型有變化，文法、拼字或標點符號無重大錯誤。
4	48	內容符合題目要求，組織大致良好，正確運用字彙及句型，文法、拼字或標點符號鮮有重大錯誤。
3	36	內容大致符合題目要求，但未完全達意，組織尚可，能夠運用的字彙有限，文法、拼字、標點符號有誤。
2	24	內容未能符合題目要求，大多難以理解，組織不良，能夠運用的字彙有限，文法、拼字、標點符號有許多錯誤。
1	12	內容未能符合題目要求，完全無法理解，沒有組織，能夠運用的字彙有限，文法、拼字、標點符號有過多錯誤。
0	0	未答/等同未答。

V. 口說能力測驗級分說明

級分	分數	說　　明
5	100	發音清晰、正確，語調正確、自然；對應內容切題，表達流暢；語法、字彙使用自如，雖仍偶有錯誤，但無礙溝通。
4	80	發音大致清晰、正確，語調大致正確、自然；對應內容切題，語法、字彙之使用雖有錯誤，但無礙溝通。
3	60	發音、語調時有錯誤，因而影響聽者對其語意的瞭解。已能掌握基本句型結構，語法仍有錯誤；且因字彙、片語有限，阻礙表達。
2	40	發音、語調錯誤均多，朗讀時常因缺乏辨識能力而略過不讀；因語法、字彙常有錯誤，而無法進行有效的溝通。
1	20	發音、語調錯誤多且嚴重，又因語法錯誤甚多，認識之單字片語有限，無法清楚表達，幾乎無溝通能力。
0	0	未答/等同未答。

　　凡應考且合乎規定者，無論成績通過與否一律發給成績單。初試及複試皆通過者，發給合格證書。成績紀錄自測驗日期起由本中心保存 2 年。

　　初試通過者，可於一年內單獨報考複試，得重複報考。惟複試一旦通過，即不得再報考。

　　已通過本英檢測驗某一級數並取得合格證書者，自複試測驗日期起 1 年內不得再報考同級數或較低級數之測驗。違反本規定報考者，其應試資格將被取消。

（以上資料取自「全民英檢學習網站」http://www.gept.org.tw）

劉毅英文「中級英檢保證班」

對於國中生來說，考上「初檢」已經沒有什麼稀奇，唯有在國二、國三考過「中級英檢」，才高人一等。有這張「中級英檢」證書，有助於申請高中入學，或高中語文資優班。

I. 上課時間： 台中總部：每週六晚上6：00～9：00
台北本部：每週日晚上6：30～9：30

II. 上課方式： 完全比照最新「中檢」命題標準命題，我們將新編的試題，印成一整本，讓同學閱讀複習方便。老師視情況上課，讓同學做測驗，同學不需要交卷，老師立刻講解，一次一次地訓練，讓同學輕鬆取得認證。

III. 保證辦法： 同學只要報一次名，就可以終生上課，考上為止，但必須每年至少考一次「中級英檢」，憑成績單才可以繼續上課，否則就必須重新報名，才能再上課。報名參加「中級英檢測驗」，但缺考，則視同沒有報名。

IV. 報名贈書： 1. 中級英檢公佈字彙
2. 中級英語字彙500題（價值180元）
3. 中級英語克漏字測驗（價值180元）
4. 中級英語文法測驗（價值180元）
5. 中級英語閱讀測驗（價值180元）
6. 中級英語聽力測驗（書＋CD一套（價值680元）
【贈書將視實際情況調整】

V. 上課教材：

VI. 報名地點： 台中總部：台中市三民路三段125號7F（李卓澔數學樓上）
TEL：（04）2221-8861

台北本部：台北市許昌街17號6F（火車站前・壽德大樓）
TEL：（02）2389-5212

Editorial Staff

● 主編 / 劉 毅

● 校訂 / 謝靜芳・蔡文華・蔡琇瑩・石支齊・張碧紋

● 校閱 / Andy Swarzman・Ted Pigott
　　　　 Bill Allen

● 封面設計 / 張國光

● 打字 / 黃淑貞・蘇淑玲

中級英語克漏字測驗

主　　　編 / 劉　毅

發 行 所 / 學習出版有限公司　　　☎ (02) 2704-5525

郵 撥 帳 號 / 0512727-2 學習出版社帳戶

登 記 證 / 局版台業 *2179* 號

印 刷 所 / 裕強彩色印刷有限公司

台 北 門 市 / 台北市許昌街 10 號 2 F　　☎ (02) 2331-4060

台灣總經銷 / 紅螞蟻圖書有限公司　　☎ (02) 2795-3656

美國總經銷 / Evergreen Book Store　　☎ (818) 2813622

本公司網址　www.learnbook.com.tw

電 子 郵 件　learnbook@learnbook.com.tw

售價：新台幣一百八十元正

2014 年 7 月 1 日新修訂

ISBN 957-519-530-2